'Typical, just typical,' Ross sneered, stepping into the room, big and menacing, breathing hard. 'Ignore a problem and it doesn't exist, huh, Fran? Well, Princess, *I'm* not going to ignore it. We're going to have this out if I have to——'

He was cut short by an ice-cube. It bounced off the hard angle of his chin, slithered down his chest and clattered on to the wooden floor. There was utter silence as the blue eyes narrowed dangerously. Fran swallowed nervously. She shouldn't have done that, but at least it had shut him up.

'That's the second time you've hit me today, lady!' Ross's voice was a purring threat. 'And that's one time too many.' He took another step forward.

'You stay where you are!' Fran squeaked, scrabbling among the ice-cubes, half-excited, half-terrified at her temerity, and still furious with him. She brandished a fistful of hard, icy missiles as she backed away. 'Ross, I'm warning you, I want you to take your things and get out——'

'Warning, Frankie?' he asked softly, still coming. 'Or bluffing . . .?'

REASONS
OF THE HEART

BY
SUSAN NAPIER

MILLS & BOON LIMITED
ETON HOUSE   18-24 PARADISE ROAD
RICHMOND   SURREY   TW9 1SR

*First published in Great Britain 1988
by Mills & Boon Limited*

© Susan Napier 1988

*Australian copyright 1987
Philippine copyright 1988
This edition 1988*

ISBN 0 263 75872 9

*Set in Times Roman 10 on 11½ pt.
01-0188-57349 C*

*Printed and bound in Great Britain by
Collins, Glasgow*

FOR MY HUSBAND
TONY

The heart has its reasons which reason does
not know.

Pascal

CHAPTER ONE

Ross Tarrant!

It had been over a decade since Francesca Lewis had laid eyes upon him, but she recognised him instantly. He had barely changed. He was still big and fantastically handsome, the maturity of years adding to, rather than diminishing his attractiveness.

Francesca blamed her dizziness on the shock of his sudden appearance, but the plunge of her heart and the tingle shooting up her spine were old, annoyingly familiar signs. She had always felt breathless and light-headed in his presence...even a glimpse of him used to be enough to set her off.

Ross Tarrant. Where had he been all these years? With his great athletic prowess, everyone had expected him to win fame for himself and his country in the international sports arena, but in the years since she had left Whaler's Bay Fran had heard nothing of him. Secretly she had been relatively unsurprised. It was just as she had predicted. He didn't have the drive to succeed. Everything had always been too easy for him. He had no need to stretch himself because everything he had ever wanted had always fallen straight into his lap.

Her eyes travelled up over the booted feet, up the tight, faded denims that hugged his thighs and strained across the strong hips, and over the wide expanse of rumpled fisherman's-rib sweater. God, he might have grown a bit with the years, but she could swear he was wearing the same clothes he had worn when he was seventeen!

By the time she looked up into his face she was braced against its devastating effect. His hair was darker than the teenage Tarrant's had been. It was a thick, glossy chestnut now instead of sun-bleached fair, and cut unfashionably long to brush the rolled neckline of his sweater. The nose which had once been broken in a game of rugby was, to her surprise, perfectly straight. Plastic surgery hardly fitted in with the swaggering macho image he had cultivated as the local, lovable 'bad boy'. The square jaw still did, and the eyes...those fathomless blue eyes, drooping slightly at the outer corners to give him the lazily sensual look that had plunged numerous schoolgirls into fits of delight. Francesca, too, at one time.

The memory brought her up short. 'Don't you know that it's dangerous to point guns at people?' she snapped belatedly, hoping that he wouldn't realise it wasn't the sight of the double-barrelled shotgun aimed in her direction that had frozen her with shock, but the man behind it.

His wide-spread stance relaxed, the shotgun drooping against the hand that supported the barrel, the stock resting securely in his crooked elbow. Now he smiled, the lop-sided smile that had been famous over three counties. Fran found it as endearing as a crocodile's grin.

'Not half as dangerous as what you're pointing at me,' he drawled.

Horrified, Fran realised that the underwater light, which she had switched on when she got into the spa, was still on. Ross Tarrant, standing above her, could see all...her breasts bobbing freely just beneath the surface of the steamy pool, the ribs lacing her new slimness down to the curving spread of her hips with their dark, shadowed centre. With an angry gasp she reached up and hit the light switch on the tiled edge of the sunken pool, then the bubble button for good measure, sinking deep into the water as the concealing froth drew an opaque screen over her nakedness. Oh, why hadn't she stopped to put on her bathing suit? She had been stiff and tired after the three-hour drive from Auckland and had merely dumped her luggage inside the cabin before seeking out the screened-off spa on the deck, too grateful for the luxury to question why it was switched on when no one had been expecting her arrival. She had thought the lateness of the hour and the cabin's isolation guarantee enough of her privacy.

'How dare you walk in here and threaten me?' Francesca blustered in the voice which she used to keep junior nurses jumping on the ware. 'You can just turn around and walk straight out again!'

'Uh-uh.' He shook his head, grinning, gun now pointed at the deck as he looped his thumbs into the front of his jeans. 'How do I know you won't plug me in the back?' He dropped into a grating Bogart impersonation, 'Stand up, sweetheart, and reach for the sky. I want to make sure you're not packing any concealed weapons, other than that lethally gorgeous body of yours...'

'Am I supposed to be amused by your cuteness?' she demanded stiffly. There was a time when she would have paid in blood to receive a compliment from Ross Tarrant. Thank God she had grown up! 'Is that thing loaded?' she demanded quellingly.

'Do I look stupid?' He shifted his weight, confidently inviting the negative.

'Frankly, yes!' Fran snapped, though it was far from true. As well as being a star sportsman, Ross had been highly intelligent at school, but too lazy to take advantage of it, content to coast through his lessons with minimum effort. 'Too stupid, obviously, to know that you shouldn't point a gun—even an unloaded one—at people.'

'I was out hunting possums when I saw the light on.' He looked amused at her little lecture. 'There have been quite a few thefts lately from holiday homes—with firearms among the stolen goods. It doesn't pay to be too trusting these days, especially in an isolated place like this.'

'My sentiments exactly, Ross Tarrant. Now would you mind going and waving *your* lethal weapon at some other innocent citizen and leaving *me* alone.'

His eyes narrowed at her use of his name. 'Do we know each other?'

'Unfortunately, yes.' Now that was *real* flattery, his not connecting her twenty-eight-year-old self with the shy, pudgy teenager who had proved so embarrassingly easy to humiliate. Not that he had much to go on. Her long, dead-straight hair was now permed into shoulder-length brown curls, and her recent illness had given her cheekbones for the first time in her life. The blue-grey colour of her eyes was too uncertain to be memorable and, in any case, Ross Tarrant had good reason *not* to want to remember Francesca Lewis. It gave her pleasure now, to remind him.

'I'm Francesca, Francesca Lewis. I've come up from Auckland to settle Grandfather's estate.'

'Francesca?' His thick brows shot up and then snapped down again as his humour quickly died. The blue eyes were filled with a speculative contempt that made Francesca bristle. Did he still bear a grudge after all these years? He had, after all, only got what had been coming to him...

'Well, well, well...' The brown-sugar voice burned acrid with mockery. 'Princess Lewis in the flesh. Should I genuflect?'

The nickname had never been an affectionate one, and Fran was dismayed at the defensive prickle it evoked. Suddenly she could feel the steam heating the sweat beading her damp face and knew that it was time to get out of the water. But she couldn't, not while he was standing there looking down at her with such bold scorn.

'I don't care what you do, as long as you don't do it here,' she said hollowly, blinking to try and dispel a sudden wave of dizziness that she knew, this time, had nothing to do with his disruptive presence. 'Would you mind going away while I get out?'

For a moment he didn't move, his eyes on her steam-wreathed head, then he squatted down, putting the gun carefully aside and frowning into her flushed face.

'Are you all right?'

'No, I'm not all right, I want to get out.'

'Feeling dizzy?'

'A bit.' She hazily resented his demand.

'Is this your robe?' He lifted the towelling wrap off the railing that ran around the wooden deck and stood up again, shaking it open for her. 'Come on. Unless you want me to come in there and give you mouth to mouth. If you faint, you'll go under.'

'Just leave it there and I'll get out when you go,' she said weakly.

He made a rude noise. 'Princess, I'm a full-grown man. I've seen more naked women than you could shake a stick at.'

'I'll bet you have!' Annoyance momentarily cleared her head. She wished now that she hadn't turned on the deck light. It was directly above his head and made it look as though he was wearing a halo of light. Ross Tarrant, angelic? Preposterous! 'I don't suppose you've changed much in that respect. The boy most likely to score, weren't you, both on and off the field?'

'And you were the girl most likely to stay on the shelf,' he reminded her brutally, his eyes flickering briefly to the ringless left hand that clutched the tiles. 'Prediction right, I take it?'

She glared at him. 'I have better things to do with my life than be some man's domestic slave.'

'Ah, yes, the selfless career...'

'At least I have one. What do *you* do for a living?'

'At the moment, nothing.'

'Huh!' She would have said more, but suddenly his face was all hazy again.

'We can't all be model citizens, Princess, and in my experience it's often the model citizens who are the worst hypocrites——'

Fran had been unaware of her head, like her thoughts, drifting downwards, until she suddenly felt cold, hard hands grasp her upper arms, completely encircling the overheated flesh and hauling her unceremoniously out of the water. His left hand slipped as he lifted her out on to the decking and they staggered for a moment in an ungainly dance, almost falling. Fran didn't have time to be embarrassed about her glistening nudity, for Ross Tarrant stooped and picked up her thick robe, wrapping her up in it without glancing at her body and plucking a towel from the deckchair for her hair.

'You're hurting,' she complained as he briskly rubbed the sodden mass.

'At least you're alive to feel. You've been ill, haven't you?' She nodded reluctantly. 'Don't you know better than to lie around in hot water when you're not up to par? And you a nurse!'

He leant over, keeping a supporting hand on her shaky frame, and twitched the pool cover back into place. Then he pushed her across the deck and through the sliding glass doors into the warmth of the cabin.

'Get into your night things and wrap up warm.' He gave her a little shove. 'I'll put my gun away and stoke up the fire.'

Fran went unsteadily into the small bedroom to find her long, practical nightgown and thick blue robe. It was a measure of her state of mind that she hadn't even noticed the new pot-belly in the corner of the living-room when she had arrived. She looked at herself in the mirror. How had Ross known that she was ill . . . because of her slimness? A militant sparkle entered her eyes. Francesca had battled plumpness for most of her life and she was proud of her current lack of weight, even though she was resigned to it being only temporary. As soon as she was fully recovered her natural metabolism would reassert itself and repad her five-foot-seven frame with its over-generous curves.

Now, you go out there and get rid of him, she told herself sternly. Be gracious and polite, but firm. The trouble was that her darkened eyes and nervous mouth gave the lie to her confidence. Ross Tarrant was an uncomfortable reminder of an embarrassing naïveté and, what was more, she sensed he knew it.

She sighed with relief when she finally ventured out to find the cabin empty. Calling it a log cabin was a bit of a misnomer, she thought, as she crossed to warm her hands over the pot-belly. Although the exterior was constructed of split-logs, inside it was more like a luxury apartment, completely panelled in native timber, thick scatter-rugs softening the gleam of polished-wood floors. With twin beds in the bedroom and two lounge-settees in the open-plan living area it could comfortably sleep six. The kitchen was spacious and well equipped, opening out on to a small, covered deck at the back and the separate bathroom and laundry, which meant that summer residents didn't have to track sand through the house when they wanted to shower off after a swim. It was usually only in summer that the cabin was rented out. In the winter it was closed up, for Ian Lewis had been determined to preserve the unspoiled nature of the few acres he had retained when he retired from farming.

Intent on some melancholy memories, Fran was almost startled out of her skin by a movement behind her.

'It's only me.' Ross Tarrant closed the back door and hefted a cleaned fish on to the tiled kitchen bench which jutted out to form a breakfast bar. Using a wicked-looking curved knife he began to expertly fillet the fish.

'I thought you'd gone.'

'You mean, you hoped I had,' he informed her with annoying perception, and she tightened the cord of her robe nervously as she noticed the frying pan heating on an element on the stove, and the flour and butter and seasonings standing ready on the bench.

'What do you think you're doing?' she demanded sternly.

'Fixing dinner.'

'Dinner!' Her voice was thin with dismay. She should have known that Ross Tarrant would delight in up-setting her.

'That meal you have in the evenings,' he added help-fully, intent on the flashing knife. 'I caught this off the beach earlier. You haven't eaten yet, have you?'

'Now, look here——' She stopped, suddenly thinking that he seemed very familiar with the layout of the place, and very cool for a man who had been ordered off the premises. 'Did you have some sort of an arrangement with my grandfather about using the facilities here?'

'Some sort,' he conceded unrevealingly, and her frowning eyes drifted from his handsome face to his busy hands. Odd that such square, solid hands could wield a knife so delicately. She had seen surgeons at work who were clumsier, men whose hands were pampered and cared for, not brown and weathered like Ross's.

'Well, you must realise that things have changed since he died,' she said with what she thought was patient reason. 'I'm going to be staying here for a week or so while I settle things with his lawyer, so you won't be able to come and go as you like, though of course you can still use the beach...'

'Why, thank you, ma'am,' he drawled, with an excessive humility that made her flush. She hadn't meant to sound condescending, only to make it quite clear that she wanted her privacy. Her grandfather hadn't actually owned the little curve of black sand just below the steps of the front deck, but he did own all the land which surrounded the beach. Locals, of course, took for granted their right-of-way. Did that mean that Ross still lived here, Ross of the itchy feet and the big plans to travel? It was his younger brother, Jason, who had wanted to stay in Whaler's Bay and take over the family crop-dusting business when his father retired.

'Why don't you take your catch home and eat it there?' she suggested, assuming that the Tarrants still lived a few kilometres down the road. Nothing much changed in Whaler's Bay. But Ross didn't satisfy her veiled curiosity.

'And if I don't?' he asked, dipping a thick fillet in flour and shaking it.

'I'll——' What? Even arguing with him made her feel exhausted, and the idea of using physical force was ludicrous. The black wool of his sweater rolled over impressively powerful shoulders and tapered down to a hard-looking waist. His sleeves were pushed up to his elbows, displaying muscled forearms covered with dark brown hair.

'I'll . . . I'll call the police and have them remove you,' she said foolishly, suddenly noticing another new addition . . . a telephone on a low table in the corner.

'If you mean Jack Trent, go ahead, then we'll see which one of us gets kicked out.' Jack Trent had been the sole police presence in Whaler's Bay for at least twenty years, and Fran wasn't surprised to discover he was still on the job. She was surprised, though, by Ross's unconcern.

'Why should *I* get kicked out?'

'Because, Princess, you're not the ruler of this castle.'

'Not——? But . . . this is Grandpa's cabin. Of course it's going to be mine!' she stated starkly.

'Is it? Or did you just assume it would be? Actually, your grandfather said he was leaving the place to me when he died.' Ross calmly put the prepared fillets into sizzling butter and pushed them around the pan.

Outrage blazed in Fran's eyes. 'To *you*? I don't believe it.' He had to be lying, she was *counting* on being heir, had committed herself on the strength of it . . . 'If you think you can just come along and appropriate *my* inheritance you've got another think coming!'

'I didn't just "come along",' he interrupted her curtly. 'I've been living in this cabin for months—leasing it. Ian and I got to know each other rather well during that time, and when I said that I'd be interested if he wanted to sell, he said that he wanted to hang on to the cabin but that I could have it when he died. He promised, in fact . . . in front of a witness, too.'

'Grandpa wouldn't do that!' Fran retorted fiercely, ignoring her own uncertainty, seeing her lovingly planned future dissipating like smoke around her ears.

'Cut out his own grandchild? Why not? You certainly did your best to cut him out of your life. It didn't seem to occur to you that Ian was a lonely old man after

Agatha died.' He gave her a look of contempt. 'You're something else, you know that, Princess? You take on a caring profession like nursing, but you don't seem capable of caring on a personal basis. I guess you thought the old man didn't deserve your attention because he wasn't sick. Well, I have news for you, Sister Lewis! Ian said he was diagnosed as having a heart condition years ago, and was having angina attacks even before your grandmother died.'

'I never knew, they never told me,' said Fran, stiff with guilt and resentment, familiar companions both. The estrangement hadn't been totally one-sided, but she didn't see why she should have to explain the painful details of her life to Ross Tarrant.

'You never gave them a chance to tell you. You always were a stuck-up bitch, too good for the rest of humanity.'

Stung by the reminder of the extreme shyness that had been misinterpreted by her fellow pupils, Fran drew hersef up to launch a volley of her own. 'And what made you suddenly so all-fired interest in my lonely grandfather's welfare? You were never loaded down with much responsibility yourself, as I recall. Could it be that you thought you might get something out of it . . . like this cabin?'

She froze at the stillness of his expression, remembering the teenager's hot temper, but when he spoke it was with a coldness that matched the ice-storm in his eyes. 'Be careful when you start casting stones, Francesca. Your own motives don't seem to be too pristine. You didn't even bother to come up for the funeral, but you're pretty quick off the mark when it comes to settling the estate.'

'I've been ill,' she snapped, angry at having the tables turned.

'Too ill even to send a wreath?' The blue eyes were deeply sceptical.

'As a matter of fact, yes!' It gave her satisfaction to tell him. 'Just after I got the telegram about Grandpa's death I collapsed. I've had pneumonia and complications...'

'All the more stupid of you to lie around in an outside spa in the middle of winter,' he stunned her by saying, completely undercutting her anger with his apparent concern. 'Were you hospitalised? Are you still on medication?'

'Yes...and none of your business,' she snapped, even more disturbed by his concern than by his contempt. 'And as for the property, when I spoke to Simpson, Grandpa's lawyer, he said that there was no will. That means that everything will automatically come to me as the only relative.'

'Not necessarily,' he punctured her smugness. 'Simpson seemed to think that the verbal promise would probably stand up in court if it came to that.'

'You've *spoken* to him?' Francesca frowned, wishing now that she had stopped off in Whangarei to appraise the lawyer of her unexpected visit. But his letter informing her of the lack of a will hadn't mentioned any possible problems and, as it had been nearing dusk by the time she'd reached the city, she had decided to press on through the last half-hour of winding roads to Whaler's Bay. She still had the key to the beach cabin, and had naturally assumed that it would be empty at this time of the year. There had been no question of staying at the old farmhouse on the hill which had been her grandfather's home, since the lawyer had told her it had been almost completely destroyed by the fire which had coincided with the old man's death. 'He can't be your lawyer, too,' she objected. 'That would be a conflict of interest.'

'We were both at the funeral, so naturally we talked. In case you don't already know, I was the one who called the fire brigade that night. I was out here on the deck when I saw the smoky glow over the hill. Thank God I'd got Ian to put in a telephone here. I made the call and raced up across the fields, but although I got there before the volunteers, it was too late. The old place had gone up like tinder and there wasn't a hope in hell of getting to Ian.'

'I'll bet there wasn't...' Guilt and resentment uttered the sly sneer and Francesca closed her eyes briefly in horror and self-digust. She wasn't really surprised to feel Ross grab her wrist and drag her against the hard edge of the bench. She opened reluctant eyes. His were glittering slits, the ridge of his cheekbone dark with angry blood. A rasp of whiskers coated the rigid jawline, emphasising his tough masculinity, and Fran felt a frisson of fear.

'If you intend to sling mud like that you can do it in a court of law, and back it up with more proof than just your avaricious insinuations,' he grated rawly. 'You know damned well that the coroner's report stated that your grandfather died of a heart attack before that electrical fire ever started. Or are you going to suggest that *he* was in on a conspiracy to murder?'

'I...I...' Francesca licked her lips, knowing he was due an abject apology for her unwarranted bitchiness, but choking over the words. She strained against the iron fingers, breaking the grip only when he let her.

'If I had doubts about keeping this place, you've banished them,' he told her grimly. 'Ian said that you never pretended to like coming back, and that you were bound to sell out to the highest bidder. Have you thought what that'll mean to the people who live here? No? He shrugged contemptuously at her flush. 'I thought not. Well, I can't stop you turning over the top twenty acres to some greedy, get-rich-quick developer, but I can sure as hell stop you getting your hands on this beach.'

'We'll see about that!' Fran turned on her heel and marched unsteadily towards the bedroom. She wanted a fair price for her land, but she wasn't out to rape the enviroment, for goodness' sake!

'Where are you going? This fish is nearly done.'

Jolted, Fran turned and stared. Did he really expect her to sit down and share a meal with him, after what they'd just said to each other? 'I'm going to get dressed. If you won't leave, *I* will. I'll get a room at the Bay Hotel until I can get an eviction notice.'

'My lease isn't up yet, Princess, and you're not going anywhere at this time of night, in your frame of mind, with a storm settling in. That's a treacherous road back down the cliffs. You'd be over the side in no time.'

'You can't stop me!' Fran's anger overrode her normally strong common sense.

'Can't I?' There was a chink as he dangled her car keys from his hand. He must have picked them up from the top of the fridge where she had tossed them when she had arrived.

'Give them to me, please,' she said firmly, resisting the urge to dash over and wrest them physically from his taunting fingers.

'In the morning, when you've calmed down.' He grinned at her fury and pushed the keys into his jeans pocket, sucking in a breath to get them past the straining denim hip. 'Of course, if you're determined to get them...' He trailed off suggestively, and Fran swallowed her rage as she toyed with the idea of accepting the challenge.

But, eyeing the outline of her keys so close to the zippered fly of his jeans, she knew she didn't dare. She imagined having to thrust her hand into the tight pocket and wriggle it down the angle of his groin to reach the keys. Oh, he would love that! And it would remind her of that other time she had struggled with his tight jeans, of his groans of delight and her illicit sense of power. Oh, *damn* this weakness! She could feel her limbs trembling with fatigue and it galled her to admit that he was right, it would be foolish to try and leave now.

'I'm not eating with you,' she said flatly, as a feeble attempt to reassert her authority, and his grin widened. He shrugged and thick, mahogany lashes screened the blue eyes as he slid the crisp, golden fillets of fish from the pan on to a platter garnished with lemon slices and bread and butter. Fran felt her mouth water treacherously and her nostrils twitch at the tempting aroma as he carried the platter over to the kauri slab table that dominated one half of the living-room. She noticed that his movements didn't have quite the old fluid grace. He must be just over thirty now, perhaps he was beginning to pay for the many follies of his youth . . . and probably his adulthood, too!

He sat and began to eat hungrily, ignoring her hovering figure until he had finished his first two pieces of fish. It flaked gently as he ate, lemon juice glistening on the crusty surface.

'Come on, Princess,' he jeered softly, when her hunger became embarrassingly obvious. 'Come down off that high horse and eat.'

She could have gone out and got her own carton of food supplies from the boot of her car, but Francesca found herself sitting down opposite Ross and allowing him to dish up a second plate.

The fish was juicy and tender and meltingly good, but although Fran ate hungrily she was too furtively aware of her companion to enjoy it. Just being in the same room with him made her feel like a gauche fifteen-year-old again, and that led her on to remember the last time they had been alone together, in the cramped back seat of a car...

'No!' Fran clenched her teeth in an effort to keep the heat from her face as she realised that she had yelped the denial aloud. She stood up hastily and carried her plate to the kitchen, avoiding his gaze as she cleared her throat. 'I...I'm tired...I think I'll go to bed now.' She was too nervous to care about being rude. Let Ross do the dishes—he had been the one to insist on making the mess!

He studied her agitation curiously for a moment then shrugged. 'Suit yourself.' He began to swab up the juices from his plate with a folded piece of bread.

'I've been using the bed by the window,' he added as she crossed the room with jerky steps, 'so I'll keep it if you don't mind.'

Sleep in the same room? Fran felt her stomach knot. She opened the bedroom door and paused as she noted the sturdy lock on the inside. She turned, and gave Ross a primly triumphant smile. 'As a matter of fact, I do. Since *you're* the temporary guest, you can sleep out here.'

She leant against the locked door and grinned at the memory of his disgusted expression. The wisdom of years might have dictated that she forgive Ross Tarrant for the adolescent humiliation she had suffered, but that didn't mean that she had ever forgotten it!

She froze as the doorhandle twisted experimentally against her back. 'It's locked,' she said unnecessarily, her voice high-pitched with apprehension. What did she really know about the man out there?

An exaggerated sigh buffeted the door. 'Well, at least pass out some blankets for me. It's going to get a lot colder out here before the night's through, and we've only got a limited amount of firewood left.'

Fran chewed her lip as a distant roll of thunder backed his claim. He *sounded* resigned, but...

'Promise you won't come in if I open the door?'

'Francesca——' He sounded more impatient than annoyed, and Fran decided to risk it. She opened one of the divan drawers and took out three thick blankets, then added the pillow from the window bed to the pile. She unlocked the door and thrust the blankets at Ross. His sudden move to take them made her shy nervously. The blankets fell between them, pushing the door open.

'What in the hell did you think I was going to do?' he growled irritably, and Fran flushed. His face took on a sudden, mocking derision. 'Surely you don't imagine that I'm so hard up for a woman that I'll leap on anything remotely female?' He grinned at her reaction to his subtle insult. 'Look, Princess, I may have been a bit raw in the old days, but I've acquired a bit of polish since then. In fact, to set the record straight, my life is overcrowded with willing women.' His grin widened and Fran had the inescapable feeling that she had overlooked some vital point. Why did he look so thoroughly amused? 'Women are always ringing me up at all times of the day and night, begging me for attention, taking off their clothes for me at the slightest suggestion. It's one of the reasons I came back to Whaler's Bay, to get away from the insatiable women in my life...'

He was exaggerating purely for effect, but the trouble was that Fran's overheated imagination could well believe it. He was too handsome for his own good... and for hers. He shifted his weight in preparation to pick up the blankets at their feet and Fran jumped. He sighed.

'I can see, Princess, that you're not going to rest until I've made the obligatory attack on your virtue, so...' He reached over and swept her across the jumbled pile and into his arms.

His mouth was a shock of warmth against hers, his large hands spreading across her shoulderblades to ensure that any resistance on her part merely rubbed their bodies suggestively together.

Thinking that it would be fruitless and undignified to struggle against his superior strength, Fran suffered the tiny, stinging burn of his tongue against the corner of her clamped mouth. His hands moved with a slow, sliding pressure all the way down her long, slender back to ride the upper curve of her buttocks, his thumbs curling around to press against her hipbones. As she tried to protest at the liberty, his tongue plunged into her mouth, filling it, whipping back and forth, stroking the sensitive upper palate, burrowing into the slick moistness under her tongue, smothering her senses with male taste and smell.

Fran felt as if she had inadvertantly touched an electric fence. A warning hum vibrated through her body, setting up a sharp tingling in her breasts and shivering up the insides of her thighs until she dug her fingers into his shoulders and tried to arch away from the treacherous current.

He took the opportunity to test the resilience of her hips with his own, his hands beginning to circle in slow, kneading motions as they sank to cup her closer to the centre of his heated hardness. The scrape of his whiskers against her tender chin provided an erotic sensual contrast to the soft, moist pulse of his tongue in her mouth and Fran suddenly found herself clinging where she had pushed. The man could kiss up a storm!

When he took his mouth away, Fran found that breathing required a voluntary command from her stunned brain.

'Satisfied?' he murmured huskily, his hands moving back to the neutral territory at her waist, blue eyes alight with a surprised speculation that flustered her. 'I hope I've managed to prove that I don't necessarily take up every invitation I'm issued.'

'I wasn't issuing any invitations!' Fran shook herself free, finding it hard to articulate with a tongue that felt twice its size after the sensual battering it had received.

'No?' He cocked his head with a wicked smile as he touched a finger to the smooth skin just behind her ear. 'You're flushed...' His finger ran down to the pulse in the shoft hollow of her throat. '...Your skin is damp, your temperature and pulse rate have increased... An invitation doesn't have to be verbal to be explicit.' His lids drooped, masking the intention in his eyes. 'And if you're so hot...' he pulled the front of her robe apart with a single, swift movement, his hands crowding in to capture her breasts, encircling the little, stiff peaks that thrust against the soft bodice of her modest nightdress '...why aren't these still sweetly soft?'

He bent his head and kissed the objects of his taunt with maddening precision before scooping up his blankets and backing out the door with a final salute of laughter at her furious confusion.

'Night-night, Princess. Safe dreams...'

CHAPTER TWO

'As you can see, Miss Lewis, the lease agreement is pretty watertight and still has several weeks to run. The death of your grandfather doesn't invalidate the document; the lease will merely be paid to his estate until such time as it is settled.'

Frustration seethed in Fran's breast as she listened to the dry, precise, ponderous tones of the elderly lawyer.

Damn! She had bounced out of bed this morning, refreshed by her first solid sleep in weeks. She was a woman with a purpose, and to achieve that purpose she was willing to talk things over in a calm and reasonable manner. She was even willing to overlook Ross's arrogant, macho attempt at intimidating her last night.

She had marched confidently out to battle, only to find her opponent missing. A note was taped to the fridge, an almost incomprehensible scrawl. Typical! she thought as she squinted at the message: 'Gone fishing. PS What's with the jungle on the porch?'

Fran had shrieked and run outside. Her precious plants, how could she have let herself forget them? Fortunately the porch was fairly sheltered and none of them seemed to have suffered from their night out on the tiles, but her carelessness was most unnerving. She couldn't afford to forget such things, not *now*...

'What about this option to buy?' Fran jabbed her finger at the offending clause.

'It is only an option, Miss Lewis,' the lawyer said cautiously, seeing something of the old man in the stubborn set of her jaw. A most...determined lady. It was evident that she and Ross Tarrant had already clashed over the matter, and out of duty to his late client he felt obliged to try and smooth things over. 'All it means is that if your grandfather decided to sell within the next year, Tarrant would have first refusal.'

'It gives strength to his claim about the cabin, too, doesn't it?' Fran said gloomily. 'Here it is in writing that Grandfather approved of him as a buyer. So even if I do get the entire estate, if I want to sell straight away I have to offer that part of the property to him first.' Why it disturbed her to think of Ross living in that cabin she couldn't quite fathom. But it did.

'True, but his offer would have to be acceptable to you,' Simpson pointed out.

'You mean I could ask some outrageous price that he couldn't afford?' said Fran thoughtfully. Actually, she doubted that there was much he *could* afford, if he wasn't working. But perhaps he was banking on the generosity of his family?

'If he could prove that you were demanding more than the market price simply as a device to deny him purchase he could take you to court.' Simpson didn't try to hide his disapproval.

Francesca sighed. 'So there's no way I can get him out?'

'Not until the lease expires.'

'And what about the claim of his that Grandfather left him the cabin?' Fran abandoned the hopeless for the merely hopeful. 'How much legal weight does that carry?'

'He does have a case, although as sole surviving blood relative you have a stronger one,' Simpson hastened to add as he saw the grey eyes simmer. 'However, there is the question of estrangement. It's fairly common knowledge locally that Tarrant and your grandfather were fairly good friends, whereas you and he...' He shifted uncomfortably in his swivel chair under her cool regard, as if the spare, roomy office was suddenly too small for him '...well, it had been some time since you saw each other. And, of course, Tarrant is the sitting tenant...'

'Possession being nine tenths of the law, I suppose,' Fran said, drily, conscious that she was sinking rapidly in the lawyer's estimation.

'It could be one of the considerations in this case. Your grandfather's intent could be implied by that lease agreement. Why don't you leave it with me, Miss Lewis? I'll register your claim against the estate and have the matter investigated for you.'

In other words, go home and let the professionals handle it. Fran's fingers tightened on the document in her hand. She had the sinking feeling that if she wasn't there to keep an eye on things, Ross would have everything his own way. In retrospect it had been foolish to resign before she had the money in hand, but for once in her life Fran had been guided by impulse, eager to get all the paperwork and planning out of the way by the time she was well enough to tackle the physical labour involved. She had come this far, she had no choice now but to fight for her rights, but she had better go back to taking things one step at a time. Up until now her whole life had been closely structured, from the rigidly old-fashioned discipline of her grandparents' home, through the narrowness of life in a Catholic girls' boarding school, to the methodical order of nursing. Now that she was breaking free of the mould she must be careful not to go overboard in her enthusiasm.

She sighed, and gave the startled lawyer one of her sudden, unexpectedly warm smiles. 'I'm sorry if I seem to be a bit like a bull at a gate, it's just that...well...I've been saving for years towards a dream of mine, and this puts it all within my grasp. I never expected... I mean, I never imagined Grandpa dying. I know he was old, but he's always been so *enduring* ...' She gestured helplessly. It was still hard to believe that he was dead, so fixed was the image in her mind of him hovering: the gruff, critical arbiter of her childhood.

Arthur Simpson found himself smiling reassuringly back. He was changing his mind about his late client's granddaughter. She wasn't quite as tough and unfeeling as she tried to appear. And, as she talked about her future plans, animation chased the shadows from her eyes and the wan hollows from her cheeks. Why, she was rather pretty... very pretty, in fact, when she smiled like that, with a slightly shy diffidence that was surprising in a woman who had earlier projected such an aura of self-confidence.

'I'll do what I can to speed things along,' he promised as he ushered her out. A thoroughly nice young woman, was his final decision, if a little confused and guilty about the source of her current good fortune.

If he had known what the 'thoroughly nice woman' was thinking about on the drive back to the Bay he might have had third thoughts about his new client's character. She wasn't feeling 'nice' at all. She was brooding darkly on ways and means.

She could sink her pride and pour her heart out to Ross in the hope of gaining his understanding, or she could beat him at his own game. Fran knew which appealed more. Beating him, preferably senseless. It went against the grain to repeat an error of the past. Trust Ross Tarrant as a repository with her precious dreams? Look at what had happened last time! She frowned at the unwinding ribbon of road ahead as the years peeled inexorably back...

At fifteen she had been as innocent as a babe in arms, released by her grandparents' financial reverses from a decade at a convent boarding school to the unimagined freedoms of the local high school. Unfortunately the transition wasn't as simple as she had expected. Plump, aware of being achingly plain, Fran tried to hide her intense shyness behind a cool façade that rapidly acquired her the reputation of being 'stuck up'. The teasing and physical jostling between the sexes was also a shock. In time Fran made a few friends, but they weren't the kind she really wanted, the bright, fun kind, the kind who flocked around Ross Tarrant and his cronies. Like every other girl in school Fran had endless fantasies about Ross. At seventeen he was almost a full grown man, his reputation as the local 'golden boy' of sport allowing him to coast through his last year of school with little academic effort. His easy-going charm meant that he was forgiven his streak of wildness, and when people shook their heads over his latest escapade they did it with a smile on their lips.

Fran longed to catch his eye, but not as part of the giggling, blushing crowd of girls who hung around him. She wanted to be somebody special, to be singled out. She wanted the impossible, to shed her pudgy, spot-prone skin and tongue-tied shyness and be transformed into the kind of sleek, bubbling, pretty blonde that Ross seemed to favour.

The day that Ross Tarrant asked Francesca Lewis to the local Saturday night dance would live, reluctantly, in her memory for ever. She accepted his casual invitation with a dazed aplomb that masked her utter stupefaction. For the rest of that week she felt like a mini-celebrity, basking in the glow of acceptance generated by the knowledge that *she* was Ross Tarrant's chosen date. By Saturday evening she was almost mindless with

REASONS OF THE HEART

agonised nervousness and bliss. She had never been to a dance before, or even on a date. Her grandparents had an unswervingly strict moral code that had further set her apart from her fellow pupils, most of whom had grown up together, but evidently even they weren't immune to the Tarrant charm. Of course, the Tarrants were regular church-goers, and the dance was being run by the church social committee and her grandfather was going to take her to the dance and pick her up afterwards, so Francesca knew that this wasn't exactly a gesture of unreserved trust, but it was a start! Her first step towards adulthood.

The dance was a revelation to a girl starved of frivolous gaiety. Ross was stunningly handsome in his blue open-necked shirt and dark trousers and, although Fran briefly mourned the fact that her dress was so much plainer than those of the other girls, she was soon enjoying herself too much to worry about it. Ross made mixing in easy, he was so relaxed and natural that Fran blossomed under his attention, surprising even herself by the way that she laughed and joked and joined in conversations with shy wit. There was no alcohol, of course, but Fran felt light-headed just drinking in the atmosphere and revelling in the feeling of belonging. Ross never once strayed from her side to dance with anyone else, and sent warning glances to any of his friends who showed signs of lingering around Fran. Only later did she realise why he hadn't wanted them around. At the time she thought he was kindly buffering her, had fantasised that perhaps he was jealous. What a gullible little idiot she had been!

In her ignorance she had been flushed and happy, letting her feelings show in the way that she danced, her silky hair flying out around her. For Ross she dropped the barriers and was delighted by the sparks of interest that she thought she saw in his eyes.

As her curfew time of ten o'clock neared she almost suffocated with joy when he leaned over his Coke and said in a deep voice, his eyes teasingly warm, 'How about we go out for a little walk? It's a really nice night out there...'

Excitement knotted in her stomach as she agreed. He wanted to be alone with her for a little while! He didn't want the evening to end either! They sneaked out separately when the parent-chaperons weren't looking, but they didn't walk very far. A car was parked under the trees behind the hall and Ross took some keys out of his pocket.

'Neville said we could sit in his car, if we liked. Do you want to?'

Fran would have jumped over the moon if he had asked her to. He unlocked the door and helped her into the back seat. She sat, tense with excitement, trying to think of something to say that would help spin out the moments before she bumped back down to reality. Ross had been so warm and protective all night, quite unlike the arrogant, brash boy he was at school. Perhaps he was showing her a side of himself that he reserved for special friends...

'You know, you're looking pretty tonight,' he told her, his voice soft in the darkness of the car.

'Thank you.' She blushed. She had dieted madly all week, to not much avail, but at least her skin had stayed miraculously free of spots and she knew she had a nice smile. People always looked a bit surprised when she smiled.

'You should always wear your hair down like that. It's the colour of milk chocolate.'

'Grannie says it's untidy and I guess it does rather get in the way. But I like long hair...that's one reason why I could never be a nun,' she said shyly.

'You were thinking about being a nun?'

She laughed at the horror in his voice. 'I wasn't. But I think the school wanted to steer me in that direction, and I think that Grannie feels there are only two worthwhile careers for a woman: nun or wife and mother.'

'Francesca——' His voice was slow and doubtful, and ever after Fran wondered whether he had actually intended to kiss her or just wanted to talk some more. She liked to think, for the sake of her wounded spirit, that he was going to confess the truth and ask her forgiveness but that her eager response deflected him. He was at an age when his sexual urges were strong and easily aroused, and the chemistry between them took them both by surprise.

She turned towards him in the moonlit darkness and somehow their lips met. With her eyes wide Fran had her first taste of man, and liked it.

'Put your arms around me.' He muttered the soft order and Fran obediently complied. Her fingers felt his shifting muscles as he pushed her against the upright seat, his hands on her shoulders burning through the thin sleeves of her white dress. He lifted his mouth from hers and this time she saw impatience written on his darkened face and felt a flutter of desperation. He was annoyed by her ineptness...

'What's the matter? Don't you like to french kiss?' he asked huskily, and she stared at him in ignorant dismay.

She opened her mouth to ask what he meant and found out. She was stunned by the intimacy of it. He was putting his tongue into her mouth and moving it around, creating a moist friction which sent a hard jolt through her body.

Her hands clenched against his back as a strange, sweet ache began to seep into her muscles, investing them with a delicious, straining tightness. She pushed her tongue experimentally against his and felt a shocking delight as he abruptly withdrew, enticing her to follow into the spicy warmth of his open mouth. She did so, eagerly, trying to do to him what he had done to her. Was he feeling the way she was...all buttery and melting inside?

He broke the kiss and they stared into each other's eyes. There was a gleam of male recognition in his that stopped her breath. Then his hands were cupping her face and his mouth fastened over hers again, gentle, teasing, yet deep and satisfying too. When she trembled, his mouth tensed and hardened, gathering her in even further, stunning her with the tremors she felt in his own body, as if it was part of hers.

'You taste good, Frankie,' he murmured in thick amazement, his trembling fingers finding and stroking her breasts in a way that made her kiss him back with untutored enthusiasm. He groaned.

'Touch me, Frankie, the way I'm touching you.' He pulled her hand to his chest, thrusting it inside his shirt. Soon both hands were roving across his skin, admiring the compact strength so different from her softness, the hot silkiness that almost burnt her fingertips. The only sound in the car was their gasping breath and the soft murmurs and groans as Fran innocently poured more fuel on the fire. Her exploring hands moved down the flat stomach to where the waistband of his trousers formed a barrier, and he stiffened with a jerk that made her freeze, afraid she was hurting him in some way. His fingers were doing things to her taut young breasts that made her feel that she was going to explode. It was so sweet, so good, that when she felt him unzip her dress and pull it off her shoulders she couldn't believe that what they were doing was wrong.

'I won't hurt you,' Ross said huskily as he sensed her momentary doubt. 'I promise...I just want to see you...'

'If...if I can look at you, too,' she whispered, half-frightened, half-excited by the shaking plea in his voice. She trembled on the verge of a new and terrible knowledge.

He tore off his shirt and she saw the moonlight ripple over bone and muscle, and caught her breath at his sheer male beauty.

'You're beautiful,' she said helplessly and he laughed uncertainly.

'You're not supposed to say that kind of thing to guys.'

'But you are.' She hardly noticed his hands returning to her bodice, easing it down further until he could reach around to the clasp of her demure cotton bra.

'Oh, no——'

'Only to look, Frankie...' His mouth opened over hers and this time it had less gentleness and more passion. It was an adult kiss and it drew an adult response from her body. She felt her breasts tighten painfully against the crisp cotton, the straps bite into her soft flesh, and moaned.

'I'm not beautiful...I'm fat...' Afraid that he would agree.

'No, you're not...you're soft and curving, the way a girl should be...' He drew a sharp breath as he released her aching breasts into the cool night air and saw the tight, dark discs that crested the plump white roundness.

'I...don't think we should do this...' Fran quivered at his look, torn by the racking desire to push herself against him and the innate maidenly modesty that cried at her to cover her nakedness. But this was Ross looking at her with such an expression of longing. Ross, whom she loved with every beat of her tender young heart...

'Oh, Frankie...' His eyes rose to her face and they were black and hot and sweet. 'Can I touch you?'

His asking made it all right. He wouldn't hurt her, not Ross. She felt the pound of his heart against the dampness of his chest and nodded dumbly.

His hands traced over her fullness very lightly, then cupped her, rounding her towards him. His palms shifted to support her, scraping across her rigid nipples, causing her to arch her spine involuntarily. Her eyes fluttered closed, her head sinking against the seat as he fondled her for long, agonising minutes. Francesca felt a wild and restless growth inside her that she didn't know how to satisfy. Her hands slipped on his slick skin and fell into his lap. He gave a loud groan that startled her into pushing against the rough cloth. He groaned again and fell across her, pushing her into a lying position. Suddenly his mouth had replaced his hands on her breasts, and he was kissing and licking at her with a roughness that set off nerve-blistering explosions throughout her body. Her hands were trapped beneath his writhing hips, pressing against a growing hardness that frightened her. His body jerking against her and his mouth tugging at her breasts made her feel sick and excited at the same time. She gave a choking gasp as she felt his hand on her thigh, under her crumpled dress. She clenched her thighs together and felt a surging heat there that built with each nip and suckle of his mouth. Then, shockingly, his hand was nestling at the apex of her thighs, touching her through the thin panties. Even she never touched herself *there*. The nun's dire warnings about the consequences of letting a boy take 'liberties' rose up to terrify her even more, and yet she still felt the terrible thrill. She gave a half-sob of shame.

Looking back it was amazing that the young, sexual animal that Ross Tarrant had been had even heard that pitifully weak protest, let alone been able to control himself sufficiently to pull away, taking huge, deep, shuddering breaths as he rested his head against the cold glass of the side window. But he had, and when he had calmed down he had even helped her readjust her clothing and told her that it was all right, they hadn't done anything wrong, that they had stopped in time. Not wanting to reveal the profundity of her ignorance she had allowed the moment to pass, conscious of his strained expression and feeling somehow to blame for being so inexperienced. As they got out of the car and she saw the anger on his face she touched him tentatively.

'Ross?'

He pulled sharply away, then groaned at her expression of hurt. 'Hell, Frankie, I'm sorry...'

'I'm not.' She smiled a brave, if shaky, smile. In spite of her earlier fear it was true, but the soft glow in her eyes just seemed to make him feel worse.

'Then, damn it, you should be. Frankie, you're not even sixteen yet!' He shuddered, and suddenly fixed her with an earnest look. 'I'll tell you what, Frankie, let's forget about tonight, OK?'

'Forget?' Forget the best night of her life! How could he even ask?

'I mean, let's start all over again and take it slow. As friends.'

'Oh, yes!' She blossomed anew with a painful sweetness that made the young man fighting his own inner battle wince. Her heart was in her eyes and he felt like the lowest swine, but perhaps it wasn't too late to redeem himself.

'And look, don't tell anyone else about to-night...I...we need to talk first, OK?' He took her hand and squeezed it, and thus it was they walked out of the darkness straight into her grandfather, waiting at the door of the dance-hall with a thunderous expression on his deeply seamed face. Fran was hauled off home in disgrace and delivered of a searing condemnation of her wicked, ungrateful behaviour. She had listened to the stern lecture with eyes downcast to hide her rebellious indifference. She didn't care if she was grounded for ever! She would still see Ross at school and they were going to be *friends*. Friendship with Ross was worth suffering chilly disapproval at home...she would be a martyr to love!

A martyr to a bunch of male chauvinist piglets more like! Francesca poured mature scorn on the disturbingly vivid images of a long-dormant memory, shocked by their erotic intensity. As she bumped down the track to the cabin she told herself sternly that she wasn't going to think about the traumatic aftermath of her first date. She had long got over her girlish disillusionment, aided by the knowledge that she had got a sweet form of revenge at the time. Besides, Ross's cruelty had actually done her a favour. It had taught her that one couldn't build one's life around someone else's. Rosy dreams were all very well, but if she was to make her way in the world, to gain acceptance from her peers, she had to earn it for herself.

And she had. She had gained top marks in School Certificate that year for the entire Northland region, and devoted her restricted spare time to convincing Agatha Lewis that nursing was almost as worthy a career as taking religious orders. The beginning of the new school year had found Francesca starting on a pre-nursing course at Auckland Technical Institute, living under close supervision in a girls' hostel.

Ross had also taught her another valuable lesson. By the time that Francesca, a nervous first-year nurse, encountered her first raft of medical students, she was well armoured against charming young men who thought that plain-looking girls should be grateful for their indiscriminate attentions.

In a way, I suppose, I should be thanking the snake instead of resenting him, Fran thought with a wry grin. Her grin faded as she came into sight of the cabin and saw Ross rummaging around in the boot of a green convertible. In front of it was parked a battered-looking pick-up truck. Neither vehicle had been there when she'd left. She swung her car in beside the convertible and got out.

'Hel-lo, pretty lady.'

She thought he was being sarcastic and frowned at the white smile, then blinked, wondering if she was going mad.

'It *is* Francesca, isn't it?' he said, his smile widening, and the reason for her momentary disorientation clicked.

'Hello, Jason.' How could she have thought he was Ross, even from the back? Jason was leaner, his hair the same shade as his brother's, but cut shorter. 'My, haven't you grown!' She imitated the teasing once-over he had given her. 'I thought you were Ross for a minute.'

He laughed. 'Give me a break, I've got a few years yet before I hit the big three-O. Come and say hello to Neville and Tess. You remember Neville Wilkins, don't you?'

'How could I forget?' Fran murmured. It had been Neville's car they had used that night. 'What is he up to these days? Is Tess his wife?'

'Tess is nobody's wife... yet. But she has a Tarrant dead in her sights.' Jason grinned as they went into the cabin and Fran struggled with a ridiculous sense of betrayal. She must be some woman if she thought she could domesticate Ross. 'As for Neville, would you believe it— he's a cop, stationed in Whangarei!'

Fran burst out laughing. Neville had been the terror of the countryside in his souped-up old Zephyr, his delinquency verging on the criminal with ominous frequency. Neville, a policeman! That was almost as funny as Ross a married man...

She was still smiling when she stepped out on to the sunlit deck to greet the three people lounging in deckchairs. Ross didn't bother to get up, but Neville did, with appreciative speed as he returned her greeting.

'Hi, Francesca. Wow! Ross didn't tell me how much you'd changed. 'His hand froze in mid-handshake as he realised how unflattering that sounded. 'I mean—er— you're looking terrific.' A slight tinge of pink entered the broad face at the compounding of his gaffe and Francesca enjoyed his momentary confusion.

'Thank you, Neville,' she said sweetly. 'But I've been ill. Give me a few weeks and I'll be as chubby as ever.' She grinned to show she wasn't offended. Nursing had taught her to take insults and compliments with equal aplomb. It was only when you really cared about someone that their poor opinion could hurt.

'I find that very hard to believe.' Neville recovered his cool at her relaxed good humour. As they smiled at each other Francesca noticed Ross lean back in his canvas chair. What was he looking so suspicious about? Then it came to her—he was wondering what had put her in such good spirit. He had expected her to come back from the lawyer covered in gloom and despondency. Fran stretched her smile wider.

Neville's brawny body moved out of her sightline as he dragged up a chair for Francesca to sit on, and she got her first look at the woman sitting beside Ross. She was tall and slender, with cropped brunette hair, lovely skin and warm brown eyes. Trust Ross to have a beautiful girlfriend, thought Fran, feeling suddenly frumpy. Her eyes fell on the unmistakable diamond ring on the slim left hand and she stared in disbelief, her heartbeat flickering. So Ross had her dead in *his* sights, too!

Jason handed Fran a cup of coffee, then circled round to stand behind the brunette. 'You don't know Tess, she only came to Whaler's Bay a couple of years ago to help her uncle at the hotel. This is my fiancée, Tessa Armstrong... Francesca Lewis.'

Fran could feel herself blush faintly as she nodded hello. Why had she automatically assumed that it was Ross, not Jason, that Tessa was attracted to? She didn't even want to know the answer to that one.

'Ross has told us the reason for your visit. I'm sorry about the circumstances,' Tess said with friendly sympathy. 'It must have been a shock for you to arrive and find somebody already in residence.'

'I think it was the gun, rather than the resident that shocked me,' Fran lied with a rueful smile.

'Gun? What gun?' Jason looked at his brother with sharp enquiry.

So he hadn't told them. Why? She would have expected him to make a meal of the story. She met the brooding blue eyes. Surely he hadn't been trying to save her embarrassment. No, he must have an ulterior motive.

'Didn't he tell you?' She decided to torpedo it, whatever it was. 'Ross arrived home to catch me skinny-dipping in the spa and tried to run me off with his shotgun. Maybe I should report him to the police for careless use of a firearm,' she said to Neville, catching him out in a flatteringly lecherous survey of her body.

'Maybe I should report you for indecent exposure!' Ross fired a return volley with deadly accuracy. 'I had to haul her out and rub her down,' he told their amused audience, while Fran tried to grapple with the turning of the tables. 'Not to mention cook her dinner and tuck her in for the night.'

'This obviously calls for a lengthy investigation,' Neville grinned. 'Are you staying on for a few days, Fran? Perhaps I could question you over dinner one night?'

'I think you'll find that Francesca will be wanting to get back to Auckland,' Ross said smugly, and a flare of indignation banished any thoughts of conciliation from Francesca's mind.

'On the contrary,' she said sweetly. 'I did only plan to stay a couple of days, but Mr Simpson changed my mind.' She felt a delicious fillip of satisfaction as the taunting blue eyes narrowed, revealing a distinct wariness.

'What did Simpson tell you about me?' he demanded.

'Exactly what you expected. That you could possibly make a claim against the estate.'

'That's all?'

'You weren't the prime topic of conversation, Ross,' she said crushingly. 'We did talk about more interesting things, like the weather, and the price of fish.' He raised his eyebrows and for some reason she thought that he was amused rather than annoyed by her put-down, though his face was deadpan.

'Are you going to stay at the hotel?' Neville asked. 'They do a very nice meal these days.'

'Oh no, I'll be staying here,' Fran said, driven by a reckless impulse to find out what was under that deadpan mask. The impulse was rewarded handsomely.

'The hell you are!' Ross growled as he shot to his feet. 'I have a tenancy agreement, as you bloody well know. Surely you two discussed *that*?'

'Language, language,' Fran tut-tutted with an irritating smile. 'Tenancy, yes, but not *sole* tenancy. That wasn't specified.' It was her turn to be smug. My, he was steaming! How lucky that she had read over the agreement so carefully, looking for non-existent loopholes. 'As of last night I'm afraid that you have gained yourself a co-tenant. Me.' Three surprised faces and a furious one egged her on. 'You wouldn't turn out the grandchild of such a *dear* friend, would you, Ross? Especially in such sad circumstances? How would such callousness look to a judge? Sole relative, weak and helpless from a serious illness, and instead of compassion you threaten her with a gun, molest her and then throw her out into the cold...'

'You're about as weak and helpless as a piranha!' Ross snarled. 'What about your pristine reputation, Princess? Aren't you afraid of besmirching it by cohabiting with a commoner?'

His sneer was a mistake. Up until then, Francesca had merely been trying to annoy him, but at his use of the hated nickname her humour took a sharp turn for the worse. If her reputation was pristine among their listeners she would be very much surprised, considering how much effort he had put into besmirching it himself thirteen years ago. She stood up and returned him glare for glare. If he was going to fight dirty, so was she!

'Since I slept here last night, I'm afraid the damage is already done,' she pointed out acidly. 'If I'm going to acquire a reputation, I'd rather it was for something a little more flattering than a cheap one-night stand.'

They stood, bristling, scowl to scowl until Jason broke the tension with a laugh. 'Hey, you two, break it up! I don't think you'll have to worry too much about local gossip. People will only have to take one look at you together and they'll know there's nothing going on. I swear you look like a couple of gunfighters squaring off at the OK corral!' He looked at his watch and pulled a wide-eyed Tess up from her seat. 'Much as we'd like to stick around for the draw, we're due at Neville's sister's for lunch. Nev?'

'Huh?' The other man had been studying the protagonists and made his decision. 'Oh, sure. Look, Fran, since you *are* staying, how about that dinner? How about tonight?'

'You don't waste any time, do you?' Fran turned to meet the balm of Neville's soothing admiration. 'But yes, I'd love to,' she added hurriedly, sensing Ross's impotent anger behind her and thinking that he couldn't very well murder her if she had a date with a policeman to keep. Besides, it would be a good opportunity to find out a bit more about Ross, and forearm herself against further nasty surprises.

'Nice to meet you, Francesca,' said Tess as they left, and she seemed to mean it.

'Thanks for returning the pick-up, Jason,' said Ross impatiently, obviously eager for them to be gone so that he could rip into Francesca.

'Oh, I was also supposed to pass on a message from Mum. She wants to see you at Sunday lunch, *without fail*. And, hey, Francesca, if you're still here why don't you come, too? Mum loves company.'

'Jason——' Ross's protest came through clenched teeth and his brother's mischievous expression intensified.

'No sour grapes, now, Ross. You said you and Francesca were going to settle it all amicably.' He grinned at the flash of lightning in the stormy grey eyes and the frustrated resignation in the blue. 'And you know Mum, she's certain to want to meet the girl her son is living with!'

CHAPTER THREE

SHE wasn't running away, Fran told herself, as she nego-
tiated her city-slick shoes over the slippery, weed-covered
rocks leading around the point, hitching up her skirt to
jump the small gaps. It was just a strategic retreat. Before
she moved out of sight she looked back over her shoulder
and saw the distant figure on the deck of the cabin. Ross
had been furious and she was nervously aware that in
baiting him she had rather painted herself into a corner.
How was she to get out of it without looking like more
of a fool than she did already?

The sea, modest in its demands on the beach, was more
aggressive against the rocks, throwing up small swells
that broke and spattered her lightly with spray. It was
further than she had thought around to the next bay and
she was panting as she rounded yet another curve to yet
another tiny inlet. And stopped dead.

There, sitting on a small rock, his arms folded, was
the very man she had been fleeing from. And he wasn't
even breathing hard!

Francesca wobbled indignantly on her rocky perch.
'How did you get here?'

'I know a short-cut,' he said, and she scowled at this
subtle reminder that he knew more about her inheritance than she did. He met her glare with a lift of thick
brown brows and stood, holding up his hand to help her
down on to the sand.

'You're limping,' she noticed automatically from his
few steps. 'Maybe you're getting too old to take short-
cuts.'

REASONS OF THE HEART

She had thought he would laugh it off with a taunt in reply, he was obviously such a prime specimen of manhood, but instead he gave her a look of such dislike that she recoiled and slipped on the hard, wet surface. As she teetered he reached up and grabbed a fistful of her tailored skirt, jerking her forward into his arms. Angry at his ability to unbalance her both physically and mentally, she pushed at him.

'Let me go, damn you! I want to go back.'

'We can never go back, Francesca,' he said, giving her words a deeper meaning, but he let her go. 'Is it really just the money, Princess? Or is it specifically *me* that you object to sharing with?'

He had hit the nail on the head, driving it clean through the fleeting satisfaction she had felt that he was now doubting that she had acted from purely mercenary instincts.

'I... *Why* did he say he would leave it to you?' She struggled to whip up her anger in the face of his cool control. 'Grandpa always believed in the work ethic. Rewards have to be earned with sweated labour. He believed quite literally in the parable of the talents. I...why *you*?' She wanted him to justify himself, to give her a reason she could logically understand.

'What makes you think that I buried mine?' he asked tautly, refusing the opportunity. 'Because I don't wear designer jeans and drive an imported status symbol? Is that how you measure success, Francesca? If so, I'm sorry for you. One can have all the material trappings of success and yet still be a failure as a human being.'

'Is that what you think I am?' she was goaded into asking, as if she cared what he thought of her.

'That's not for me to judge. Unlike you, Princess, I don't estimate a person's worth on appearance.' A faint smile touched the sensuous mouth as he allowed his eyes to peruse her stiffened figure. 'If I did I would be thoroughly confused by now, wouldn't I? Are you the satin-skinned sensualist who likes skinny-dipping and french kissing? Or the neatly tailored spinster who doesn't approve of anything or anyone that deviates from her prim conception of the norm?'

His reference to french kissing was unnerving. Had it been a deliberate reminder of her youthful indiscretion, or was she reading things into his words that didn't exist? *Satin-skinned sensualist?* Absurd!

'If you really want to live at Whaler's Bay, why don't you go and live with your family... or don't *they* want you around, either?'

He merely grinned at her abrupt change of subject. 'Quite the contrary. Mum would love to have me back in the nest but I'm way past the stage, in age and experience, where I'd be comfortable there for any length of time. They're a great crowd, but they're just that, a crowd. Tess is living there until the wedding, Dave has started a rock band who seem to have taken up permanent residence in the barn and little Beth has blossomed into a seventeen-year-old beauty trailing clouds of mooning youths who clutter up the passageways. Add to that a mother who longs to have me safely married off, and a father who cons any hands idle for more than a few seconds into helping on his interminable home-improvement projects and you have some idea why I appreciate the peace of my own establishment.'

'*My* establishment,' Fran corrected firmly, 'and since when did *you* ever seek the peaceful life?'

'Ever?' he repeated mockingly. 'We were only acquainted for a shortish while, Frankie, so you can't claim that sort of knowledge. Any at all in fact—you didn't want to contaminate that dainty, narrow mind of yours by mixing with a crude lout like me, remember? Crude or not, I've lived and learned a lot since then.'

'Oh, really, learned what?' she snapped, stiffening her spine against that silky *Frankie*. Ross had been the only man to call her that. And the crack about louts came dangerously close to an open reference to that awful Monday she had tried so hard to forget. 'Learned how to con old men? Is that how you scratch a living?' She had to insult him. He wasn't going to slip past her guard by making her curious about what he had been up to in the meantime. She didn't care, except so far as it affected *her*.

His nostrils flared slightly, but there was no other outward sign of temper. Instead he squared his stance and cocked his head and said, very, very blandly, 'Women.'

'What?'

'I make a living from women.' He enjoyed her startled suspicion. 'They pay to visit me, or sometimes they ring me and I visit them. We exchange...er...intimate information and part with satisfaction on both sides. I have a lot of *very* satisfied clients.'

'You're...a...a *gigolo*?' Fran's shock and suspicion melted into distaste. She had expected something disreputable, but this...!

He gave her a smouldering smile. 'That term is a bit outdated, not to say obvious. I prefer to think of myself as serving mankind...or, in my case, womankind.'

'I...that's disgusting!' Fran spluttered.

'Is satisfying human need disgusting?' he said, feigning surprise. 'You should be the first to congratulate me, Princess. You were the one who told me I was wasting my potential.'

'I didn't mean your sexual potential!' she hissed, flushing furiously when she realised where the conversation had led her.

'As I recall, you didn't specify, but perhaps your memory is more vivid than mine,' he goaded her softly. 'No? Then let me see if I can refresh it. You told me, after making sure that half the school was listening, of course, that I was quite fun on a date, but a little too crude and clumsy for your taste. That the boys you used to sneak out on dates with when you went to that snooty girls' school of yours had much more class. Who wants to be friends with a guy on the fast-track to nowhere? you said. I was spoiled and lazy and I would never realise my potential because whatever natural talent I had would always be stifled by my even greater talent for taking the easy option...'

'I'm flattered you bothered to remember what I said,' Fran murmured stiffly, unnerved by the thought that his memories might be just as vivid as hers. 'What a pity you obviously didn't take it to heart.'

'What makes you think that?'

'Well,' she floundered, trying to come up with a reason for her reasonless conviction. 'You were just as much a hell-raiser as ever when I left, and I didn't see your name listed in the Bursary examination results...'

'Keeping tabs on me, Princess?' he needled softly.

'Nothing of the kind,' she denied, pink-faced. 'I just happened to notice.'

'I got by without.' Surprisingly he didn't pursue the blush, but he didn't hide his humorous satisfaction either. 'I decided to exploit my natural talent with women...and guided by your advice I decided not to stifle my skills by restricting myself to only *one*...'

'No wonder you don't dare live at home!' She drew in her mouth primly, unable to help responding to the provocation, even though she knew it was deliberate. Her antagonism towards the man seemed inbuilt, and drove her into uncharacteristic over-reaction. 'If you think I'm going to let you use my cabin to——'

'Rest—I told you I was after some peace. Even gigolos need holidays.' His mouth quirked as she bridled. 'Don't worry, Princess, I won't ask you for money. I doubt that, even with your inheritance, you could afford my rates!'

He was that good? Fran found herself thinking wryly, then was horrified at herself. Ross was grinning openly at her now and she didn't know whether to believe him or not. He was so damned sexy it was easy to believe that he could flatter women into paying for the privilege of his company.

'I'm not as gullible as all that, Ross,' she said, to convince herself. 'You're not going to scare me off with those tactics. I don't care what kind of low-life you are, I'm not backing down. Were you ever this "honest" with Grandpa?'

'I respected the old man too much to upset him by flaunting the differences in our philosophies in his face, but I never lied to him. At least I was there for him to talk to. He was pretty stubborn and opinionated, and set in his ways, but interesting for all that. A pity you never showed any interest. Not very dutiful of you, Fran...'

Duty. How that word stung. 'I wrote——'

His sound of disgust cut her off. She wanted to shout at him to leave her alone, and yet she knew she couldn't just walk away from his accusations. Something about him compelled her to stand up to him. She had the feeling that if she let him have any kind of victory over her, no matter how small, he might glimpse how really vulnerable and uncertain she was. Her life was already in the midst of a state of flux and she didn't know if she could handle any more complications right now.

'A few letters may have salved your conscience, but what that old man needed was *you*. You never came much, apparently, even when Agatha was alive. Were you ashamed of them? Too good for the people who took you into their home and brought you up? God, the way Ian talked it was as though you were some sort of saint! He was so proud of you... of how well you were doing and how busy you were, even if it meant you were too damned busy to take an occasional weekend off to visit an old man.'

'He didn't want my company. He never did!' Fran defended herself fiercely. 'Maybe, towards the end, he did need it, maybe I should have come, but for what? He never talked to me and I didn't know how to talk to him. I don't even know if I liked him. He certainly never tried to like me.' When she saw the protest form in the blue eyes she went on, doggedly, 'Oh yes, he and Agatha were *proud*, but not of me, personally. They didn't know what kind of person I was, they never wanted to know, they just wanted a shiny image to show the world. As long as I did what I was told and didn't disgrace myself, as long as I was *dutiful*, they never asked for more. Do you wonder I didn't like coming back here? This was never really home to me. Home is where the heart is, and there was no heart in my relationship with my grandparents, only duty.' She laughed bitterly into his suddenly still face. So he thought he knew it all! 'They were such pillars of the community. Everyone thought they were so wonderful for taking in their illegitimate granddaughter and bringing her up, but their pride gave them no choice. They *had* to take me in. And I was a constant reminder of how they had failed in bringing up their own child. I suppose they decided they had been too lenient with my mother, because they obviously couldn't trust themselves to control the taint in *my* veins. They handed me over to strangers to bring up through my formative years. I was six when they packed me off to that school. Six! The nuns were kind, of course, but they had their vows. Their love was detached, it couldn't be squandered on individuals...

Her voice hoarsened in an echo of the lost bewilderment she had felt in those early years. 'It didn't take me long to realise that my grandparents were proudest of me when I wasn't there. They even encouraged me to take my holidays with schoolfriends, rather than come back home. I'd be lonely, they said.' She laughed again, but this time it was ironic. 'Maybe they were afraid I'd contaminate *you*, rather than the other way around.'

'They were victims of their own upbringing, too.' Ross's voice was deep and slow, and full of a compassionate understanding that she didn't want to believe he was capable of. 'It can't have been easy when your mother was killed and they suddenly found themselves with a baby on their hands, just when they were looking forward to their retirement years. They did their best...'

'Best for whom?' Fran asked wearily. 'I could have been adopted by a couple who *did* want me, been able to feel part of a family instead of never being able to shake off the feeling I was here on sufferance.' She threw her head back and challenged him. 'I happen to think that they owed me more than duty, they owed me *love*. More than that, they owed it to me to accept *my* love, but shows of affection were very much discouraged. They expected the worst of me, even when I gave them the best. They never trusted me, and as a consequence I never really trusted them. I'm sorry Grandpa's dead, but I can't say I shed many tears, except for what might have been. I am what they taught me to be.' She faced him proudly, showing him that although she had explained, she wasn't apologising.

Ross shifted his uncomfortably intent gaze to the sea and the silence began to stretch. Fran felt her nerves stretch with it. She had probably sounded like a self-pitying idiot, throwing all those old resentments at him. She had never opened up like that with anyone before, not even in a temper, so why now, to *him*?

'If I offered to withdraw any claim to the cabin, would you move out and let me stay out my lease?'

Fran's eyes snapped to his face. It was totally without expression, as if he was carefully repressing his thoughts. He hadn't shaved this morning and the rough stubble along the hard jaw and untidy hair gave him a heightened air of masculinity. Fran was appalled at her sudden desire to trust him, to give in to his strength.

'No,' she said flatly, daring him to try and talk her into it.

'Surely we can reach some sort of compromise——'

'No!' Fran had been compromising her needs and emotions all her life. She was tired of deferring to other people, of doing what *they* wanted her to do. She was putting her foot down, now. 'You started this, Ross Tarrant, but I'm going to finish it. If anyone compromises, it'll be you. *I'm* staying in *my* cabin!'

'For God's sake, I don't want the damned thing...I never did!' he exploded at her.

Fran went rigid with disbelief. 'You're lying...you just want me out of the way so that you can——'

'Look, Francesca——' his voice was gritty with constraint '—*yes*, your grandfather said I could have the place when he died, and *yes*, I'm interested in buying. But I had no intention of contesting any claim until you walked in with your lady-of-the-manor act. All I knew was that you let the old man down when he needed you, and now you were strolling in to rake up the goodies. I still don't like the idea of your selling to anyone but a local, but what the hell——' he shrugged impatiently '—I'm not a local any more myself. So why don't you go back to wherever you came from and let Simpson expedite the estate for you, and just leave me in peace?'

Instead of soothing her, his curt explanation infuriated Fran even more. In the midst of a strenuous battle with the enemy she found herself punching air. How dared he think he could upset her like he had and then shrug off his deliberate obstruction as a misunderstanding! And he was actually putting some of the blame on *her*!

'You should have thought about the consequences before you started slinging threats around,' she took pleasure in telling him. 'But then you never worried overmuch about the future, did you, Ross? Only about the pleasures of the moment. Well...tough. For once you're going to have to live with the consequences: namely—me!'

She felt good as she began to scramble back over the rocks. Ross Tarrant was a symbol of the negative aspects of her life, the things she could never have, could never be. Now for the first time she felt that she was dealing with the sense of inadequacy he raised, and which she tried to hide by professing to despise everything about him, on an adult level. She wanted to hold on to this heady feeling of triumph for as long as she could.

Her confidence in having the upper hand was reinforced by having him trail, muttering, after her. When they reached the smooth sand again she noticed from a brief flick of her head that he was still limping. The nurse in her rose up.

'You'd better let me take a look at that leg of yours when we get back. You might have pulled a muscle or something.'

His rude rejoinder didn't put her off.

'Don't be silly, a person who's perfectly fit doesn't limp for no reason.'

'I fell coming down the cliff,' he snarled sullenly at her, bringing her to a dead stop, her hands automatically settling on her waist.

'The cliff? The short-cut was down that cliff?' Her eyes flickered closed as she visualised for an instant that apparently smooth clay face. 'You must be mad!'

His glare was pronounced, his face stiff with what she recognised was offended male pride. He had always had too much of it. 'I haven't got one foot in the grave yet, Princess. I've been rock-climbing half my life...and jogging, and scuba-diving, and sky-diving. I'm not one of your city-soft coronary-candidates sliding into middle age. I can take care of my body myself, thank you.'

'No wonder you don't work, you're too busy working out. Once a jock, always a jock, huh, Ross?' she mocked. 'And I suppose it isn't macho to admit that enough is enough. People who *over*-exercise have coronaries, too, you know.'

This time it was Fran who trotted behind while Ross strode on, and she took the time to professionally study the swing of his leg. By the look of him it was his left hip as well as his ankle that was bothering him.

'I don't "exercise",' he threw over his shoulder. 'I set myself physical challenges.'

'You call plunging down a cliff a challenge? I would say it was stupidity.'

'Yes, I suppose you would. You don't trust yourself any more than you trust other people, do you? You like things to be nice and safe. You wouldn't understand how

much pleasure the element of risk adds to an activity. I
don't suppose you ever took a risk on anything in your
life.'

Francesca began to laugh, and Ross stopped and stared
at her. She was genuinely amused, grey eyes dancing with
slivers of blue light, her thick caramel curls flowing over
her shoulders as she tilted her face to the sky. A month
ago his words might have been true, but at the moment
her entire life was one big risk. Was it a pleasurable one?
No, but she couldn't honestly say that she wasn't enjoying *parts* of it. Parts that didn't include Ross, of
course, she told herself, biting off her laughter as she
caught the lancing puzzlement of his gaze.

'What's so funny?' he asked, with the slightly sulky
tones of someone who hasn't understood a joke that
everyone else finds hilarious.

Fran had no intention of telling him. It gave her a
much-needed sense of security, knowing that he couldn't
read her half as well as he thought he could.

'Are you going to "risk" showing me that leg?' She
grinned smugly at him.

A tiny flame flickered in the deep blue eyes. 'I'll let
you play nurse if you let me play doctor,' he said slyly,
his grin replacing hers.

Smugness and compassion died a rapid death. Let him
suffer then! She sniffed and stalked into the cabin. He
would have to *beg* before she'd lift a finger to help him!

They lunched separately, Fran reading a gardening
manual at the table, Ross taking a repulsively large
sandwich out on to the deck. He propped his leg up on
a stool, she noticed, steaming lightly at the bull-
headedness of *some people*. After she had eaten her
dainty triangles she soothed herself by spending the
afternoon emphasising her presence: arranging her plants

around the cabin, finding the best position for each, and watering and chatting encouragingly to them.

'If you're so hard up for company, Princess, why don't you come out here? I guess I can endure some conversation. I'm certainly not getting any peace with you burbling about in the background.' Ross lowered his book to watch her admonish a Boston fern for being reluctant to grow.

'You can always leave,' she said loftily, brushing a curl away from the corner of her mouth and casting a brief look of scorn at the lurid cover of his paperback. 'I think the conversation I get in here is much more intelligent than any I might get from you.'

'Still the intellectual snob?' He was irritatingly uncrushed. 'Look, Frankie, living with someone who's a friend, or family, is hard enough. Living with an enemy would be hell on wheels. Pull in your horns, Sister Lewis, I'm through arguing with you for today.'

He took his book and went out and lay in the tall, yellowing grass that waved on the little hillocks that presaged the hills behind the cabin, his head resting against the upturned, aluminium-hulled dinghy that Ian Lewis had hardly ever used, preferring to fish from the rocks.

Time hung heavily on Fran's hands. She wasn't used to having any spare time, and the quietness was almost too intense. The sea, like rippling grass, barely whispered on the shore and the only other sounds were from the gulls and shags and terns that shared nesting places in the clifftop trees.

She took her leisure getting ready for her dinner with Neville, lingering in the shower and making-up with slow precision. It was a long time since she had gone out with a man she didn't know... a long time since she had gone out with anyone other than Brian. The hand applying eye-shadow paused as she thought of the horrendous row they'd had before she had left for Whaler's Bay. They had said bitter things to each other, but in Fran's case it had been a bitterness tinged with relief. Brian had been part of the life that had been closing in on her, and an indivisible part, judging from the comments he had made about her resignation. He didn't approve, had even accused her of going through an early mid-life crisis, and Fran had discovered that she really didn't care what he thought. Scarcely the basis of a good relationship!

She finger-dried her hair, glad to see some of the highlights returning after the lank lifelessness of the last few weeks, and fluffed out the perm to give her a carefully tousled look. The mouth that she had always thought was too narrow looked wider and fuller in the fined-down version of her normally rounded face, and the plum-coloured lipstick emphasised the difference.

She was wearing the one 'good' dress she had packed for unexpected eventualities just like this: a blue wool crêpe with a modestly plunging neckline and a skirt that warmly followed the contours of her hips and thighs. It was slightly loose on her, but Fran hadn't wanted to invest in a whole new wardrobe when she knew that she would soon be back to her old size. She looked at herself in the mirror screwed to the bedroom wall and was pleased. This would show Ross that she wasn't a starchy Sister, or a snobby Princess. She was a woman, too, and even though she wasn't beautiful, at least she didn't have to *pay* a man to go out with her!

Ross had opened a can of tomato soup for his dinner and was drinking it out of a thick mug when she walked into the lounge. He set the mug on the table, thoughtfully dunking a slice of toast into the wide mouth and chewing on it unhurriedly as he looked her over.

'All this for Neville?' he murmured at last, hiding the gleam in his eyes under lazy lids. 'Go easy on him, won't you, Princess? He's only a country boy like me; he might not know the right protocol to follow.'

Against her will Fran felt herself flush with pleasure at the oblique compliment and tore her eyes away from his handsome face to stare at the hand which held the toast. The back was covered with dark hair which ran up under the folded cuff of his sweater. She guessed that his arms and legs, like his chest, would be thickly furred. She blinked as her eyes settled on his expensive-looking watch. A 'gift' from one of his 'clients'?

'For goodness' sake, he's a grown man! He doesn't need you to run interference for him,' she said tartly.

'Even grown men have trouble figuring out women sometimes. Why are you going out with him, anyway? I wouldn't have thought he was your type.'

'And what is my type?' she was unable to resist asking.

His eyebrows rose mockingly. 'Don't you know? Dear me, Frankie, it sounds as if your love-life to date has been sadly lacking.'

'My love-life has been entirely satisfactory,' she fibbed.

'Damned with faint praise, huh?' he grinned tauntingly. 'Seems us country boys might be able to teach your sophisticated city slickers a thing or two, after all.'

'You can cut out the "down home" accent, Ross.' Her eyes sparkled with temper. 'You said you didn't live around here any more, and I scarcely think that there'd be much call for *your* kind of services in quiet rural backwaters!'

'You can take the boy out of the country, Princess...' he said mirthfully, and again she had the uncomfortable feeling that he was laughing at more than just the present conversation. 'But you're right, the pickings are richer in the cities...more women to the square metre.' He took another swig of his soup and eyed her provocatively. 'But you're very cleverly evading my question.

Never mind, we both know the *real* reason you agreed to go out with Neville...'

Fran gave him a haughty look. She wasn't going to touch that one with a barge-pole. Besides, she knew he intended to enlighten her anyway. And so he did.

'Actually there are two. The first is that you don't trust yourself alone with me...and the second is that you're dying to pump poor old Nev for information, or should I say ammunition, you can use against me.'

'You arrogant hulk!' Fran snapped, furious that he had caught her out in the latter, and insulted her by the former. 'It's *you* I don't trust.' She thought of adding that he left her cold, but the words suddenly stuck in her throat. Also, his gross male ego might take it as a challenge. 'I happen to think that Neville is an extremely attractive man.'

Her dignity cut little ice. 'Oh, sure, and you have no intention of even *mentioning* me during your hot date.'

'Why should I spoil a nice evening?' Fran flared. 'But maybe I ought to warn him about how you make a living, if he doesn't already know. The police might want to issue a warning to people to lock up their daughters.'

'And wives,' he told her with outrageous cheerfulness. 'And mothers and grandmothers. No woman is turned from my door.'

'Except those who can't afford your fees,' she said, certain that he was exaggerating just to rattle her. With his looks, Ross could probably pick and choose his 'clients' very carefully.

'Oh, I do a certain amount of charity work,' he laughed. 'Ask Neville. I bet you won't be able to resist. Admit it, you're as curious as a cat about me. Why don't you just forget about going out with Neville and stay home with me? That way you cut out the middle man.'

A flash of headlights shone through the kitchen window and rescued Fran from a fast degenerating situation. 'That's him now,' she said with visible relief, taking the cabin key from the top of the fridge and putting it in her slim clutch bag. 'We might be late, so don't bother to wait up for me.'

'Don't do anything I wouldn't do,' he chuckled, toasting her with his mug.

'That *really* narrows the field down, doesn't it? Sarcasm dripped from every syllable as she threw open the kitchen door and stepped outside, pursued by his laughter.

'Ten bucks says you won't get through the night without giving in to your insatiable desire to know me better, Princess!'

The throaty challenge rang in her ears as she greeted Neville's appreciative hello. Unfortunately he had heard Ross's laughter, if not his comment, and, as she got into the car, asked her what the joke had been. The date was only five seconds old and already the subject was that wretched man. Well, she would eat poison before she would let him be proved right! She would forget all about her insufferable house-guest and just enjoy her night out.

It wasn't easy. The consciousness that she wasn't going to mention his name kept in the forefront of her mind, an invisible third person at the dinner table, monitoring her conversation. In spite of that, the evening was pleasant. In a way, Neville reminded her of Brian; they both had the same, rather complacent view of their lives stretching ahead of them, from point A to point B, like a neatly kerbed and well sealed highway. Fran, who had just taken an abrupt turn on to a sharply rutted side-road, felt the faint stirrings of impatience even as she enjoyed the comfortable tenor of Neville's unthreatening flattery. He was obviously interested in seeing her again, but Fran was politely non-committal. She had just escaped one dead-end relationship; she didn't want to embark, even briefly, on another. She needed to reserve her energy for more important things...

'...coincidence that you're both up here from Auckland convalescing at the same time. Did you ever run into each other in the big city?'

Francesca suddenly registered what he was saying, and her firm resolve vanished on the instant. 'Has Ross been ill?' she enquired sharply.

'Didn't he tell you?' He looked surprised, then grinned. 'I suppose he's fed up with all the sympathy—he was always so savagely healthy, I guess being laid up has been driving him crazy. Remember that time he broke his nose? The coach had to practically manhandle him off the football field. Never say die, that's Ross's motto.'

'How——?' Fran took a sip of wine to stop herself forming the question. If Neville chose to tell her she would listen, but she would not *ask*.

'Sky-diving,' he obliged genially. 'His 'chute tangled and wouldn't detach, and so did his emergency. Smashed himself up pretty badly...oh, about four months ago, I think it was.'

'He was lucky even to survive,' said Fran, tight-lipped, her surge of horror overtaken by anger. If he was convalescing, what was he doing sliding down cliffs? Not that his pig-headedness was anything she could control. She felt thoroughly sorry for the doctors and nurses who had looked after him; he had probably made their lives hell. Or, in the case of the nurses, heaven—the traitorous thought sneaked into her mind.

Determinedly she managed to get through the rest of the evening with her curiosity under tight rein. In a complete volte-face she decided that she didn't need to know anything personal about Ross Tarrant—she didn't *want*

CHAPTER FOUR

ROSS TARRANT lowered his book and stared broodingly towards the clatter in the kitchen which had penetrated his concentration. Francesca was attacking the evening dishes as though to leave them a second longer would herald the death of the civilised world. His eyes moved from the set of her shoulders to the long line of her back. Apart from its uncomfortable stiffness it was rather a sexy back.

His connoisseur's eye slid to the swerve of her hips, recalling how she had looked nude and steamy, flushed and feminine in her weakness.

He frowned. Three days ago it had seemed such a simple, foolproof plan: drive out the irritatingly neat Sister Lewis by driving her up the wall. But the foolproof plan had backfired. He was the one quietly going up the wall!

How could one woman be so infuriatingly obstinate and yet so easy to manipulate? He lifted his book again to hide a slow grin. It might be childish of him, but he enjoyed fuelling her misconceptions about him. She was so deliciously easy to provoke into a passion that belied that prim exterior.

His grin faded. There was the rub. He was curious about her. Before she had turned up, the peace and quiet had begun to pall and yet he had known he wasn't ready, physically or psychologically, to ease back into the swing of his life. Thwarting Francesca had been in the nature of a diversion that, once his initial temper had cooled, amused his restless mind. He had not felt in the least guilty. Francesca had proved that she could look after herself, and at least she came alive at his taunts. Flaring back at him she didn't look quite so much like a wind-up doll marching stiffly towards some predetermined fate. He was doing her a favour, loosening her up.

Liar! he told himself disgustedly. His motives were entirely selfish. He never could resist a challenge and Francesca was the most flagrant one he had come across in a long time. What marvellous irony to be penned up with one of the few women who had ever rejected him outright! Actually, Francesca had the distinction of being the first, and as such had earned herself a special place in his memory. For another reason too, one that she would no doubt be astonished to hear, but he intended to save the telling until the right moment. She had earned the embarrassment. It might teach her a little humility to realise how gullible her rigid thinking made her. And in the meantime he wanted to explore the fascinating perversities of human biology.

To his amused chagrin Ross had realised that the old chemistry still existed and that, if he was any judge of body language, it wasn't only one-sided. Fran was giving out unmistakable signals to a man who had built part of his professional reputation on his ability to read and interpret the nuances of female expression. She resented the undercurrent of attraction, that much was obvious, and he shared her reluctance. Francesca was not the sort of woman he sought out for male/female games. He liked women who were frank and open about their de-sires and emotions, women who preferred lovemaking to fighting, who were fun to be with and didn't tax his patience by demanding too much of his valuable time. Francesca was the total opposite. She was rather like a locked room ... perhaps the female equivalent of Black-beard's lair, he speculated mischievously, littered with the bodies of past unfortunates who had been chewed up and spat out by that discreetly sexual, but tightly controlled personality. What was the key to Francesca? he wondered. What might he release if he found it? He had the time, but did he have the inclination—or the courage?

Francesca was aware of the strange vibrations from across the room. What was he thinking about? New ways to drive her up the wall? Surprisingly he hadn't even mentioned her date with Neville. Instead of baiting her mercilessly about his bet he had greeted her the next morning with a slightly expectant silence. She had ignored him until driven to point out that he hadn't even bothered to wash his few dishes from last night's dinner, adding snidely that perhaps he might find work as a dishwasher if nothing else. That had restored his acid humour and it hadn't faltered since.

Francesca had to concede that she had overestimated her ability to outstay him. As a nurse she had frequently lived in shared accommodation, but fellow nurses were quite different from a *man*. A man, moreover, who didn't want you there, who had no sense of organisation, who was sullen and uncooperative and didn't seem to know one end of a broom from the other. The only other man that Francesca had lived with had been her grandfather, and he had been a rigidly correct man who never came to a meal unless he was fully dressed, and liked everything to be in its rightful place.

Ross Tarrant was a creature of impulse. He slept when he was sleepy, ate when he was hungry and had a disconcerting habit of walking around half-naked. He was untidy and inconsiderate and refused to share the chores.

Francesca had caught on very early. He was doing it deliberately. No one could be that slovenly and not have died of some certifiable disease years ago!

She extracted her revenge by carrying her desire for neatness to obsession point. The fact that her constant nagging of him to tidy up got on her own nerves as well as his was beside the point, although sometimes she forgot entirely what the point was supposed to be!

Francesca was drying the last dish when the telephone rang. She turned automatically. Although Ross was well within reach of the phone it would be just like him to let it ring and ring until she was forced to answer it. But this time she had misjudged him.

'Tarrant.' He listened for a moment. His eyes shot to Fran and a devilish grin lit out across his lips. 'Yes, you have, and she is here, but she's just...er...got other things on her mind at the moment, if you know what I mean...'

Propelled by that leering innuendo Fran scooted across the room and grabbed at the receiver. Ross fended her off from his chair with mocking ease.

'Who am I? Her live-in boyfriend. Who are you?'

'Stop it! Give that phone to me!' Francesca hissed furiously, rushing in under his guard and wrenching the phone away from him. 'Hello?'

'Hi, Fran. Who's the hunk?'

'Oh, hello, Christina.' She had rung her friend from the lawyer's office to let her know of the hiccup in their plans. Christina had been less upset than Fran, pointing out that they couldn't do anything anyway until the Council had made up its mind about the Change of Land Use application, and the bank had officially notified them of their loan approval. 'No panic, just relax for a few days. You need it,' had been her cheerful advice.

'Look, I can call back if you and the hunk are——'

'We're certainly not!' snapped Fran, giving her tormentor a killing look. 'That was his idea of a sick joke. He's just a co-tenant, that's all.'

'Pity, he sounds nice.' Like a true friend Christina took the hint in Francesca's terse reply and dropped the subject. 'I just called to let you know that the Council came up trumps. Now we only have the loan to worry about.'

'That's great!' Fran's face lit up, her whole body expressing delighted relief to her interested audience. She listened while Christina brought her up to date with the rest of her activities, feeling buoyant again after the frustration of the past few days.

'Doug and I had a spat, and Brian phoned, full of remorse, wanting to know where he could reach you. I told him, politely of course, to bug off.'

'Thanks.' Christina had never really taken to Brian, although she had always been pleasant to him.

'Perhaps I should tell him you're living with someone up there. That should ram home the message.'

'No, thanks,' Fran shuddered. Things were complicated enough. She looked at Ross, unashamedly listening, and buoyancy made her rash. 'I don't think he'd be very impressive, he's the immature pretty-boy type.' Ross's eyes narrowed as he realised who she was describing. 'He fancies himself as a lady-killer,' said Fran gleefully, 'but he's handicapped at the moment... smashed himself up in a sky-diving accident. He's pretty seedy all round, but I guess when he's not sulking or flexing his beach-boy muscles he has a certain frayed charm.'

She hung up on Christina's laughter, suddenly nervous at the smug look that Ross was directing her way. He didn't look at all disturbed by her insults.

'Who told you about my accident?'

Dammit, she had forgotten she wasn't supposed to know! She flushed guiltily, turning on her heel and fleeing back to the kitchen. Ross followed her crowing with triumph.

'You owe me ten bucks!'

'Oh, no, I don't.' Fran grabbed the dishcloth and began wiping the bench diligently. 'I never bet. *You're* the gambler around here.' She'd been waiting thirteen years to make that taunt, but of course it sailed right over his thick head.

'And what other titbits of information about me did you wheedle out of my unsuspecting chum?'

'I didn't *wheedle*. He mentioned it, that's all.' She crossed her fingers in the folds of her skirt. 'That's the only time I even thought of you all night.'

He grinned so jauntily she wanted to hit him. Instead she poked a stick into his weak spot. She had noticed how impatient he was for total recovery, it showed in the way he pushed himself and stubbornly refused to make concessions to his injuries or admit to feeling pain, snarling at her if she dared comment.

'How long do you think you'll have to take it easy? What will you do when you're completely recovered?'

'I'm practically recovered now,' he was quick to answer, scowling at her.

'Maybe you'd better think about finding yourself a proper job, then,' she said scathingly. 'Your old one might not support you in the style to which you're accustomed. You might find that women baulk at paying top price for damaged goods.'

She saw his mouth tauten on a quick intake of breath. 'Bitch,' he said softly. 'That was below the belt.'

Francesca was suddenly ashamed. How could she, a nurse, an *ex*-nurse, mock someone's affliction? It went against every principle of her training, as well as violating common human decency. It was just that he made her so mad!

'I'm sorry,' she said gruffly, avoiding the sudden darkness of his eyes. 'Er...what *were* your injuries, anyway?'

He continued to look at her for a moment in silence, as if to judge her sincerity, then leaned on the breakfast bar and told her, with an almost clinical detachment that both fascinated and repulsed her. He was talking about *himself*, not some nameless textbook case.

'I was lucky that I landed in bushy scrub which cushioned my fall; I was lucky, in fact, that most of the breaks were clean. I had a compressed fracture of the vertebrae but there were no complications. It's my left arm that's the problem, a vertical fracture of the humerus is pretty difficult to deal with.'

Fran wasn't interested in technical details, she was trying to cope with a rush of complex emotions—fear, relief, a bewildering empathy with his pain. 'You're lucky to be alive at all, let alone walking around,' she said shakily.

'I know,' he said gently, sunning himself in the brief warmth of her compassion. 'It's going to make the next jump that much more difficult.'

'You're going back up, after what happened?' Fran was milk-pale in disbelief. How could he risk putting himself, his friends and family, through that all over again?

'I have to.' He smiled wryly at her blank incomprehension.

'Weren't you warned?' she asked feverishly. 'Didn't the doctors tell you that there'll probably always be a slight weakness on that side——'

'What thoroughly boring, predictable lives we'd all lead if we allowed ourselves to be governed by *probably*,' he replied calmly. 'You wear blinkers, Princess, if you think you can make life safe by sticking to the straight and narrow. Hasn't your profession taught you that one can never be completely safe, that death, disease and accidents are appallingly random?'

'It's taught me a certain amount of fatalism,' she said, not entirely truthfully. When you're busy carving your own fate, fatalism doesn't have quite the same meaning.

He sighed and shook his head. 'Princess, you need drastic loosening up. You need to relax, or you're going to turn into one of those arid, iron-skinned, sour-tongued martinets that nurses and patients alike love to hate.'

What would he know? Francesca gave him a sharp look. Perhaps he had had one on the ward he had been in? It was on the tip of her tongue to tell him that officially she was no longer a nurse, but he would probably give her that wretchedly smug grin and make jokes about abdication. And then he would ask what she was going to do and be even *more* impossibly smug that she was doing exactly as he told her she should.

She couldn't quite put her finger on it, but that conversation seemed to mark a turning point in her relationship with Ross. His teasing became lighter, lacking the sullen, threatening undertones it had had since she had announced her decision to stay. However, instead of making her relax it made her more suspicious of him than ever, convinced it was merely a ruse to lull her into thinking he no longer cared whether she stayed or went.

Impossible as it seemed, Ross became even more casual around the cabin, until every crevice appeared to harbour evidence of his inhabitance: a discarded sock under the table, *Sports Digest* magazines migrating from room to room, shaving foam on the mirror, and food—he always seemed to be eating—which he would put down somewhere and then forget about. He was always mildly apologetic when Fran pointed these things out to him, but he never changed one iota until at last she gave up nagging and resigned herself to cleaning up after the worst of his untidiness and resolutely ignoring the lesser irritations.

It seemed silly to prepare food separately, so they worked out a tacit arrangement whereby Fran provided breakfast, they got their own lunches, and Ross cooked the dinner. He was a far more imaginative chef than she was, not to mention a better cook, and Fran found herself thinking that if they lived together much longer she would have to start worrying about dieting again. She had no scales to weigh herself on, but just by looking at herself in the bathroom mirror she could see her ribs filling out.

Sometimes Ross would bring back his fishing catch for a meal and every now and then he would disappear in his rackety pick-up and return from a tour of the local roadside produce stalls laden with garden-fresh vegetables. Fran made sure that the expense of their bought food was strictly shared. She had no idea what the state of his finances were; perhaps he was slipping into Whangarei on his outings to collect his unemployment benefit cheque, or perhaps he was still on Accident Compensation? Anyhow, once or twice he visited his parents and came back with a pie or a casserole, so perhaps his family were helping make ends meet. How awful, to be thirty and still living such an apparently meagre existence, she thought with a shudder. At least she would always have her training to fall back on. She might lose her savings in this new venture, but she need never be destitute.

The weather over the next few days continued warm and sunny, unseasonably so, and Ross had taken to stripping down accordingly. The first time Fran walked in and saw him standing there, dressed only in tight, cut-off denim shorts, she almost had cardiac arrest. He was behind the kitchen bench, the shorts slung so low on his hips that at first she had thought he was naked. There were a few scars and still some signs of deep tissue bruising, but even so he had a beautiful body! Fran could only see slight signs of softening from his months of curtailed activity.

'Does my body embarrass you?' He had raised innocent eyebrows at her dropped jaw, forcing her to reach for nonchalance.

'Of course not, I've seen better.' A valiant lie. 'You've got a bit of weight settling in, haven't you?'

To her delight he scowled. 'I'm working on it.'

He got his revenge that evening as she sat by the fire, reading one of his awful paperbacks with a frown on her face and a certain guilty fascination with the machinations of the rich and promiscuous characters. Ross usually took a long, relaxing spa after dinner, and tonight he wandered through with only a towel hitched around his hips, apparently to fetch a magazine.

As he bent to flick through the stack on the coffee table, Fran couldn't help seeing the towel part where the edges were rolled over at the hip, revealing the solid thigh flowing into his flank, the pale flesh there smooth and hairless in contrast to the thick dark coating on the strong legs and wide chest. He straightened and turned so that she was now staring at the front of his body, at the dangerous dip across his belly which showed the triangle of hair which faded to his navel, thickening out again below it. He sauntered casually over to stand boldly in front of her, magazines tucked under his arm.

'You don't seem very interested in that book. Want to come and join me?'

'No, thank you,' she said quickly, too quickly, mind tensing from the impact of all that bare male flesh.

'Come on, Frankie,' he wheedled. 'Don't be shy. You told me that nurses were blasé about nakedness. Or is it *your* body that embarrasses you?' His voice became infuriatingly earnest. 'I know you're pretty skinny at the moment, but from the glimpse I got the other night you still have lovely breasts. Not as big as they used to be, but still nicely shaped. That's one of the things I remembered best about you, your——'

'Will you shut up?' Francesca threw the book aside, her face red with embarrassment and temper. 'We both know that I was fat. Fat and plain. I admit it, OK? You've got back at me for this morning, so let's just forget it now, shall we?'

The tormenting mockery left his face, but Fran was too busy staring hard at her feet to notice. 'You weren't fat, you were plump and the plumpness was in all the right places. I know that thinness is fashionable, but it flies in the face of human physiology. Women are *supposed* to carry extra pads of fat, their bodies are designed to have curves. I personally prefer a woman to look as nature intended her to, rather than to force herself into a fashionable strait-jacket of skin by excessive dieting or the offices of some quack plastic surgeon.'

Fran's eyes flew to his face, and away again, a warmth spreading through her body as she realised he was utterly sincere. It was all the more believable because he hadn't disputed her claim to have been plain. They both knew that she had been.

'Who are you to call plastic surgeons quacks?' she said teasingly, to hide the embarrassed pleasure she felt. 'Or am I mistaken that you've had your nose fixed?'

To her amusement Ross's hand flew to his nose and he actually flushed, forgetting he was supposed to be menacing her with his gorgeousness. 'Well, yes, but it wasn't my idea. The guy who did it got me to sign the form while I was still bleary with drugs after my first operation. He did the nose job before I realised what was going on.'

Fran was horrified. 'That sounds like a serious breach of ethics. Who was it?'

'Er...a personal friend,' Ross seemed uncomfortable. 'He'd been nagging me for years to get it done.'

'He should have left it the way it was,' said Fran tartly, when it seemed he wasn't going to enlarge on the statement.

He raised his eyebrow with a return of humour. 'To stop me from being stuck with the 'pretty boy' label? Do you think I'm *too* handsome, Princess? I assure you, I may be pretty, but I'm all man...'

The low, masculine purr made the hairs on the back of Francesca's neck rise as she watched, dry-mouthed, as he ran a caressing hand across the rippling muscles of his chest, down over the hard, slightly concave belly to the tuck of his towel. She jerked out of her chair and backed away from that awesome body.

'Oh, go and have your damned spa!' The warmth of his laughter followed her into the bedroom where she slammed the door and stood trying to control her breathing. Involuntarily her hand moved to cup her breast, and she flushed as she remembered his admiration. At fifteen she had been shocked as well as excited to discover how sensitive she was there. Her next sexual encounter, several years later, had reinforced that discovery, disappointing as the affair had been in almost all other respects, including her ultimate satisfaction. In fact, that short flirtation with modern sexual mores had persuaded her that she was one of those women who didn't have a particularly strong sex drive...or so she had thought until now! But then, she had never met a man who exuded blatant sexuality the way that Ross did.

She must try and conquer this silly habit of getting hot
and flustered by his suggestive teasing, that was what he
wanted ...

The next morning she ignored his insufferable good
humour at the breakfast table and took herself off for
a leisurely walk, hunting for interesting pebbles on the
beach. Idly she thought how nice it would be to spend
a little time every now and then in such peaceful sur-
roundings. Was there some way that she could perhaps
keep the cabin and ...

She stopped short, dropping all her carefully collected
pebbles with a faint sound of dismay. Perhaps there was
a way, but it would mean even more juggling of finances,
and negotiating with the bank and perhaps trimming
back on her capital investment. No, better to sell. A
holiday home was hardly on the list of her priorities ... it might be years before she had the time, or
the spare cash, to take enough holidays to warrant one.
Besides, a naughty voice whispered, without Ross
around, the peaceful life would pall pretty quickly ...

'What are you doing? Put that down!' she ordered
tightly when she got back to the cabin and found Ross
had taken it upon himself to shift around some of her
plants. It seemed symptomatic of their relationship, Ross
acting and she reacting.

'What does it look like I'm doing?' said Ross mildly,
holding the maidenhair fern from the coffee table out
of her reach. At least he was wearing a shirt this morning,
even if it did have some interesting holes in it, matching
his tattered jeans. 'I'm putting some of this greenery out.
It's shedding into my coffee. If you were only coming
up for a few days, what did you want to lug all these
things up here for?'

'I couldn't ask my neighbours to look after *every*-thing. Anyway, the ones I brought were special. Some of them are quite rare and others need specialised care.'

'This isn't rare. Even I know what this one is, it's as common as grass.'

'It happens to be going through a rough patch,' said Fran, managing to snatch the offending, offended plant and set it gently back down on the table. 'Plants don't just need food and water, you know, they need company, too...'

'You can't really believe that!' He was laughing at her, as usual.

'I happen to *know* it,' she said haughtily. 'I've done experiments on my horticultural course to prove it. This little fern was ailing until I began to chat to her every day. Now she's starting to perk up.'

'She?' He looked from plant to Fran, his face a study of disbelief. 'You divide your plants into *sexes*?'

Ross would bring sex into a discussion about rocks! 'A lot of plants put out male and female flowers on different bushes. If you want to cross-fertilise you need to know which is which.'

'And this is female?'

She flushed at being caught out. 'Well, I could hardly call a *maiden*hair "he", could I?' She was unaware she'd put her hands on her hips and thrust her chin out challengingly. So she talked to her plants and invested them with personalities, so what? It was a harmless eccentricity. If he thought her crazy for talking to her plants, imagine what he would think if he knew that she was about to devote her life to them? He would be rolling on the floor. Sister Lewis, nursing plants rather than patients...he would tell her that it was because plants were no threat to her—they couldn't answer back.

She built an effective case against herself that was abruptly demolished when he said mildly, 'No, I guess not. Did you propagate all these yourself, or do you haunt the garden centres?'

Yes to both questions, she was tempted to reply, one garden centre in particular, but she contented herself with, 'I like to grow things from scratch, there's more satisfaction that way.'

'Only pot plants, or do you have a garden?'

'Sort of.' She hesitated but, seeing only interest in the blue eyes she continued, 'It's not really mine, it belongs to the whole block where my flat is, but it's enormous and nobody else takes much of an interest so...'

'So it's yours.'

She smiled a little sheepishly, grey eyes shifted to a deeper, warmer shade, her mouth curving to soften the pale contours of her face as she told him how she had slaved over that piece of land, planned and plotted and landscaped to her heart's content, until it had won a local Garden Beautiful contest. The landlord had been blasé, until he discovered that the improved environment could entitle him to put the rent up when new tenants moved in. Pointing out to him that he had outlaid nothing, therefore couldn't claim increased costs to the Rent Commission, Fran had bullied him into a business arrangement.

'It sounds as if you have green fingers. Must be a good way to work off the stress of your job.'

Her eyes took on an intriguingly secretive glint of amusement which made him probe gently, watching as she blossomed with enthusiasm, her gestures wide and sweeping, her body held confidently, her mouth mobile with pleasure. This was how he liked her to look.

'You really are a nature baby, aren't you?' he teased gently when she ran down and began to look abashed at her childish enthusiasm.

'I suppose so,' she murmured, wondering what she had said to put that curious expression on his face. It was almost . . . tender. Her eyes dropped to see his hand stroking through the maidenhair.

'Don't do that,' she said involuntarily, disturbed by the sexual symbolism of the gesture. Would he run his fingers through a lover's hair like that?

'Why?' A forefinger lifted a tiny, delicate leaf so that it lay submissively on the tip. He leaned forward to inspect it, his breath stirring the other leaves, his other hand cupping a trembling frond on the far side with a gentleness that, absurdly and totally illogically, seemed highly erotic. He looked up at her silence, the hazy blue eyes fusing with hers. 'Jealous?' he asked softly, as if he could read her mind. 'Of a *plant*, Frankie?'

'Maidenhairs bruise easily,' she said huskily, thinking that she should summon anger at the arrogance of the taunt, but drawn instead by the silent message in his eyes.

'So do people, Princess,' he said, confirming the message. 'Shall we agree not to bruise each other?'

Francesca didn't answer. She couldn't. She had the frightening feeling that it might be already too late to escape her reacquaintance with Ross Tarrant totally unscathed . . .

CHAPTER FIVE

'COME on, Francesca, jump! I'm not going to wait around here all day.' Ross sounded thoroughly fed up.

'I can't, it's too far.' Fran hated the slight whine in her voice. She was fed up with him, too. It wasn't enough for him that they were out in the fresh air. Oh, no, Ross always had to go that extra distance, round the next point or over the next ridge. Looking down at the sea boiling into the crevasse below her, and Ross impatiently waiting on the rocks on the other side, she decided that enough was enough.

'I can't do it.'

'There you go again. Every time I ask you to make a little extra effort it's the same: I can't! Until I *make* you.'

'Little?' Fran exploded at him, trying to force the tangle of curls out of her eyes as the wind whipped them to a froth. 'I don't call this *little*. "Let's go around the rocks," you said. You didn't say you were taking me mountaineering!'

'Don't exaggerate, Fran,' he drawled, with a grin at her flushed face and heaving breasts.

'This kind of thing may turn you on, Ross Tarrant,' she said bitingly, unreasonably annoyed by that masculine gleam. 'But I don't find it at all exciting.'

'What kind of thing?' He leaned his shoulder against the rock, as if there was a square kilometre of solid ground beneath his feet instead of a narrow ledge above a three-metre drop to some treacherous seas.

'Danger,' Fran gritted at his handsome, dangerous face.

'It's not really dangerous, if you know what you're doing.'

'But I *don't* know what I'm doing!' she wailed with a shiver. Down on the beach it had been warm, the sun high in the sky, but up here the wind cut through her sweater and chilled her skin.

'I do, and that's all you have to worry about,' he said complacently. 'Now jump, sweetie, and I'll catch you.' He held his arms wide, bracing himself with one hip and knee against the rockface.

'What if I fall?'

'I won't let you fall.'

'What if you can't help it?' she persisted. 'You know your shoulder's still weak. What if your arm gives way?'

'It won't give way.' Some of his impatient humour died and she regretted reminding him of his weakness. It had been fear finding an outlet but, from his brooding expression, he thought she had done it deliberately. 'Are you going to jump? Because if you're not, you can damned well stay there.'

'You wouldn't leave me!' Fran exclaimed accusingly, looking behind her and remembering all the encouragement she had required to get *this* far.

'Wouldn't I?' he smiled grimly. 'A no-good layabout like me? If you fell, there'd be no one standing between me and the cabin, would there?'

'Oh, don't be ridiculous,' she snapped, fingers digging into rock as she looked nervously down. Neither of them had mentioned their dispute for days and he had to bring it up now!

'My, my, Princess, we have progressed. At one time you intimated that I had murdered your grandfather for his property. Have you changed your mind?'

'I . . . I was angry, I didn't mean it,' she said sulkily, adding, with immense reluctance, 'I'm sorry. *Now* can we go back?'

'A handsome apology,' he said softly and her flush deepened.

'I *am* sorry . . . I . . . you make me so angry sometimes I forget myself . . .'

'Or, sometimes *remember* . . . mmm?' he said with unnerving accuracy. His voice became coaxing instead of challenging. 'I would never have brought you round this way if I really thought you couldn't do it, Fran.'

She wavered, knowing she was being silly, but unable to make the move. How did he know what she could or couldn't manage, when she wasn't sure herself? 'I'm going back,' she decided firmly.

'You can't. The tide will have covered all those convenient stepping-stones we hopped across on our way around the point. You have to come this way, you haven't got any choice.'

'You didn't tell me this was a one-way trip!' Fran screeched at him. 'How do we get back? Swim?'

'A little further round there's a reserve that comes right down to sea-level. It's a gentle stroll up the hill and across the fields to home from there.' He was unmoved by her spluttering fury. 'I didn't tell you because I knew you wouldn't come if there wasn't a comfortable option for you. Now, are you going to jump or do I go on without you?'

'You wouldn't dare!' The unwise words were out before she could stop them. There was an infinitesimal silence, then he smiled, a predatory-shark smile.

Fran stared furiously at the place where he had been. She waited apprehensively for him to reappear around the corner after he had considered he had taught her a lesson. He did not return.

Apprehension turned to fear, then to anger. If she fell and broke her neck it would be entirely his fault! How dared he take risks with her life the way he did with his own?

Anger is a great motivator. When Fran jumped it was with a full head of boiling steam. Clutching frantically on to the rock face as her feet steadied on the ledge Fran felt a furious sense of triumph. When she looked back, she was chastened to discover that during her leap the chasm had shrunk...it wasn't *that* wide or high. Achievement had reduced what fear had magnified. Still, he had no right to make her do it!

She was even more annoyed when she edged around the corner and discovered that Ross wasn't smugly waiting there, just out of sight, ready to fly to her resuce if need be. He really had gone on! Breathing heavily, she struggled on around the rocky spur for what seemed like an age.

She came upon Ross eventually, sunning himself like a seal on a flat rock in a sandy inlet riddled with caves. He had stripped off his shirt and draped it over his face, his jean-clad legs stretched out so that the grubby sneakers hung over the edge of the rock, the soles lapped by the tide. At shore level the wind was no more than a gentle breeze, and Fran could feel the sweat trickling down the neck of her wool sweater.

'You pig!' she attacked his peaceful indifference. 'I could have fallen back there!'

A lazy hand lifted the shirt from his face, the muscles in his arms flexing under a light sheen of sweat as he propped himself up on an elbow, eyes slitted against the sun. 'I knew you wouldn't let yourself fall, Princess. You were too anxious to give me the sharp edge of your tongue to worry about mundane things like falling.'

'Well, you had more confidence in me than I did.' She suddenly felt weak and wobbly, and didn't know whether it was from delayed fright or the sight of that crisp pelt of red-brown hair catching the sunlight and playing it over his well developed chest. His jeans, as usual, rode low on the lean hips.

'I think that's your problem, Princess. Your self-confidence has gaping holes in it . . . it makes you prickly and defensive.'

'I don't need any of your rockside psychiatry, thank you, Dr Tarrant,' she said sarcastically, but he only chuckled indulgently.

'Admit it, Princess, you got a big thrill out of besting me and that damned crevasse.'

'I hate you, Ross Tarrant——' she began heatedly, wondering why, considering the lengths he had driven her to over the past week, she was still on speaking terms with him.

'No, you don't, you just hate it when I'm right,' he said with lazy perception, lying down again. 'Take off your sweater and get some sun. You could do with some extra Vitamin D, and you're far too pale.'

'Fear tends to do that to me,' she muttered blackly, but she did what he suggested, lying beside him on the rock after first making sure there was ample space between them. The hard warmth at her back, and the soft caress of sun on her exposed skin soon melted away her ill-temper. Perhaps she did need to be prodded out of her native caution once in a while . . . but not too far and not too often! As if he sensed her softening, Ross began to talk about some of the places he had travelled to during his apparently peripatetic life . . . places that Fran had only dreamed of seeing. He didn't satisfy her curiosity as to how he had afforded his travels, and she didn't ask.

'It sounds as if you've been just about everywhere,' she said wistfully, not opening her eyes. 'I've barely travelled around *this* country.'

'You have to take your chances when they come . . . or make your own. Nurses are always in demand overseas. Or why don't you use some of your inheritance and take a trip?'

'I already have plans for that.'

'Oh, what?' She heard his head turn, felt his gaze on her sun-warmed face, and took pleasure in denying the curiosity she heard in his voice.

'None of your business.' She smiled, the movement making jagged red patterns on the inside of her eyelids. To the man who had propped himself up beside her that secretive smile was an alluring challenge. He had a sudden desire to burrow inside that mysterious contentment of hers and lay her bare to his senses. To strip away the defensive barriers of her mind, as well as her clothes, and satisfy both curiosity and libido at the same time.

When there was no comeback to her provocative remark Fran opened her eyes. Ross's long, half-naked body was suffocatingly close, the expression on his face as unidentifiable as it was disturbing. She sat up, tucking her legs protectively against her chest and clasping her arms around her blue corduroy-covered knees.

'I suppose, on these great travels of yours, you pursued your usual obsession for danger. Did you conquer the world's natural wonders? Ski the Alps, swim the Rhine, climb the Eiger . . . ?'

His face relaxed into teasing lines. 'Dave is the mountaineer of the family, not me . . . he's planning a Himalayas trip next year . . . and most of the Rhine is too polluted to swim, but I definitely skied. Nearly got caught in an avalanche once, as a matter of fact.'

'You would,' Fran grumbled. If he wasn't looking for danger it was obviously seeking him. 'What is so attractive about dangerous sports?'

'It's not the danger *per se*, although as you just discovered that does generate a certain exhilaration in the bloodstream. It's the challenge of testing oneself, of discovering just how far one can push one's limitations.'

'But . . . to risk life so *casually*——' She struggled to understand.

'I'm far from casual,' he said, sitting fully upright so that his hip brushed hers. She edged away from the scalding contact. 'I use all the necessary safety precautions and I never tackle impossible odds.'

'Is it your courage you're trying to prove? Your fearlessness?'

'I don't believe that courage *is* fearlessness,' he said, tilting his proud head to the sun. 'I think that courage is far more than just an absence of fear, or a reaction to danger. I think courage is *resisting* fear, acknowledging and mastering it instead of letting it master you.'

His philosophy was unsettling to Fran, who thought fears were far better tucked away out of sight and, if possible, forgotten altogether. The man himself was a challenge to everything she thought and felt. More than a challenge—a threat. He seemed to have the ability to persuade her to do things that she really didn't want to do, undermining her initial refusals with a mixture of logic and teasing that never failed to ignite her normally controlled temperament. In fact, she realised with horror as she trailed him back to the cabin, he had her seeking his approval, acting like a lovestruck child instead of a mature woman who needed no one's approval but her own!

Francesca looked about her with fresh eyes when they got back to the cabin at last, and she was aghast at the evidence of Ross's influence over her better nature. The clutter was verging on mess . . . and she had even allowed herself to fall into his habit of leaving the dinner dishes until the following morning, and even then to merely wash and leave them draining on the bench!

Alarmed at how quickly her natural discipline had been undermined, Francesca punished herself with an orgy of cleaning that, over the next twenty-four hours, sent Ross into spasms of mocking abuse which culminated, the next afternoon, in a trivial but fiercely escalating row that sent him storming out of the cabin, declaring her to be a neurotically obsessed personality with delusions of sainthood.

'Better than having delusions of godhead!' she flung after him, pleased at having pierced his easy-going skin. 'Only gods are invulnerable, Ross Tarrant, but you'd rather kill yourself than admit it!'

When the cabin was aggressively sparkling Fran stomped out of it herself, finding the pleasure in his absence was short-lived. She had thought of some magnificent put-downs to his insults and he wasn't there to hear them. He was always going on and on to her about accepting people the way they were and not imposing *her* expectations on them. What about him? Wasn't *he* trying to change *her*, imposing expectations of his own?

She glared at the sight of Ross in the dinghy, rowing vigorously across the bay. He could row to China for all she cared! She tried skipping a few stones, failing miserably. Another lesson of Ross's that hadn't taken.

When she looked up again Ross had stopped rowing and was leaning back in the dinghy, letting it drift. He was several hundred metres off the beach now, slowly moving towards the point. The sun, which had promised another jewel-like day, had reneged and slid behind a flowering cloud which was turning the sea grey-green.

Ross began to row again but this time, instead of moving smoothly, the dinghy began to spin in circles. Fran frowned. What was he doing now? He was acting like a complete amateur. The drift seawards continued and her scathing thoughts disappeared in a puff of smoke as she suddenly realised that he wasn't kidding around. Something was wrong.

If he drifted out past the point into the channel, the current would take him God knew where...and he hadn't a hope of making it to the rocks unless he got control of the dinghy. His arm! Of course...typical Ross, so convinced of his physical prowess that it never occurred to him that his arm might not be up to rowing a heavy dinghy.

Fran tried to shout out, but the breeze which had sprung up took away her breath, the same breeze that was creating tiny white-caps on the choppy water. She felt an instant's panic as she wondered what to do. Should she run in and telephone for help? What if the weather suddenly changed for the worse in the meantime and Ross got swamped? What if he wasn't in trouble at all? He would be furious if she humiliated him by calling out the coastguard for nothing.

Her eyes measured the distance. Three hundred metres? Easily within reach. Without a second thought she stripped off her slacks and jumper, carefully placed her watch on top, and ran down into the water, not even flinching as the frigid waters closed around her, her eyes fixed on Ross, still going around in circles, still drifting. The fool! The blind idiot! She would tear him into strips!

It wasn't until she was half-way out that she began to feel the cold. She stopped, treading water for a moment, noticing with a leap of fear that the distance between them seemed to have widened rather than narrowed.

What if she got cramp? Ross wouldn't be able to help her. What if he kept drifting, just out of reach?

She refused to go back. She gritted her teeth and put her head down and swam. She alternated strokes as she felt herself tire, trying not to think about cramps or sharks . . . it was too cold for sharks, wasn't it? So intent was she on not dwelling on the awful possibilities that she almost swam into the side of the dinghy, banging her hand painfully on the hull, only to have it grabbed even more painfully.

'What the *hell* do you think you were doing?' Ross yelled at her as he hauled her roughly into the bottom of the boat. Gasping for breath Fran stared up at the pale, thunderous face. 'What a bloody stupid thing to do! That water is like ice. Are you trying to extend your sick leave by getting another bout of pneumonia?'

Fran was shaking, but it was with combined shock and rage rather than cold. 'You were floating out to sea!' she yelled back at him as she sat up. 'Talk about being bloody stupid! What did you take the boat out for in the first place? You *know* your arm isn't up to sustained activity like rowing. I thought you never tackled impossible odds.' She snatched the oars and began to row furiously.

'I could have managed,' he said tightly, trying to take one oar. 'You didn't have to risk your fool neck——'

'Shut up, Ross Tarrant. Just sit there and shut up!' She spurned his effort to help furiously. She didn't feel the wind chilling her skin, she didn't feel the rivulets from her hair streaming down her shoulders, she wasn't aware of the wet transparency of her bra and panties. She was sustained by sheer temper.

The silence was a solid wall until they reached the beach and hauled the dinghy up on the sand above the high-water line. Ross's face was stiff and pale, his eyes shuttered as he watched her bundle up her clothes and start jerkily towards the cabin. Then she stopped and turned on him, unable to help herself.

'What is it with you, Ross? Was this another test to put yourself through? Do you have a death-wish or something? You weren't even wearing a *life-jacket*——'

'Why don't we continue this discussion *after* we've dried off?' Ross interrupted her tersely, plucking at his spray-damp shirt as he took in her huge eyes in a frozen face, the thick lashes meshed with salt. 'You need a shower, and a session in the spa to warm up.'

Suddenly feeling too exhausted to argue, Fran stumbled away. The shower felt like hot needles piercing her skin and yet not warming her. It was with a shudder of gratitude that she sank into the spa and felt its comforting heat seep into her aching bones.

Ross appeared on the deck wearing a towelling robe that skimmed the tops of his thighs. He was carrying a tray which he set down on the tiled edge of the pool.

'What's that?' She looked suspiciously at the bottle and two glasses.

'Brandy. For shock.'

'I'm not *in* shock.' A moment later she was, as he shrugged off his robe and stepped down into the water. Confronted with a naked Ross Tarrant, sculptured muscle from head to foot and supremely unself-conscious of his undeniable maleness, Fran's brain went into overdrive. She gaped, blushed, paled and closed her eyes. When a glass was thrust into her trembling hands she gulped it indiscriminately. It was like swallowing molten metal. Her eyes flew open and stung with tears, blurring the image of him sitting calmly across from her, waves lapping at the solid slope of his shoulders as he sipped his own brandy.

'You're suppose to sip it,' he told her gravely.

'Don't you tell me what to do! Don't you *ever* tell me what to do, not after——' She clenched her teeth and stared at him with fierce eyes. Defiantly she tossed back the rest of the brandy, trying to ignore the way it peeled the lining from her throat, and held up her glass. He poured and she drank that too, to make her point. Ross was no longer pale, but there was still tension around his mouth and a kind of quiet resignation in his eyes that made her feel very odd. Or was it the brandy?

'Why?' She whispered suddenly and he sighed as if he had been braced for the question and actually welcomed it.

'I'm sorry, Princess. I was in a temper and out to kick the world in the teeth. It was a very dumb thing to do and it put you in danger. Forgive me?' He was very, very quiet and Fran gulped, taking a grip on her anger. It was the only thing holding back the tears.

'Even a child would have had more sense.'

'I agree.'

'You could have floated out to sea and drowned.'

'I know.'

'And *I* would have felt responsible.'

'I'm sorry.'

'And will you stop being so humble?' she shouted at him. 'It doesn't suit you at all.' She slopped some more brandy into her glass, frowning when it brimmed over into the steamy water. Suddenly she wasn't angry any more, she was sad...so sad. Tears welled up and she didn't have the strength to stop them. She sniffed. 'I was so scared...'

She heard a vague clink as he put his glass down. 'Oh, Frankie, so was I...I knew that I wouldn't be much use to you if you got into trouble...I couldn't even help myself...this damned arm!' His voice relaxed again as he took her glass away and cuddled her close to his side. 'Don't cry, darling, we're both safe...safe and warm again.' He nuzzled her mouth reassuringly, his broad arms scooping around her back so he could stroke her gently. Fran forgot her sadness as her breasts were crushed against the silky-wet hair of his chest. She wriggled closer, blissfully revelling in the movement of skin on skin, and he gave a wry half-groan against her cheek before his mouth found hers. The kiss was long and deep and slow, and it made Fran's brandy-muddled head rock. In fact, the whole world was rocking.

'I think I feel seasick,' she murmured languorously, not at all dismayed. 'Do you think I should have some more brandy?'

'Definitely not.' He closed her eyes with kisses and when she opened them again after another pleasant sea journey she found herself back in the cabin, swathed in towels, on a rug on the floor in front of the fire. Ross was beside her, back in his bathrobe, with her nightgown and robe slung over his arm.

'It's too early to go to bed,' Fran protested dreamily.

'You don't have to go to bed, but you're not going out again. The weather's closing in, so you may as well put these on.'

'I can't, I'm too weak,' she slurred smugly. Lead weights on her hands and feet prevented her from moving.

'Are you asking me to put them on for you?' His face held mingled amusement and wariness, confronted with a wide-eyed, kittenish woman who aroused his protective instincts as well as making him aware of baser ones. It was a Francesca at once strange and disarming.

Emboldened by brandy, she gave him a slow up-and-under smile that he couldn't fail to mistake.

'Sit up.'

She sat up obediently and watched with interest as he slowly unwrapped the towels. There was silence as they both looked down at her body. Ross drew a long, unsteady breath as he unfolded her nightgown.

'Do you think I'm pretty?' Fran demanded, offended at his lack of reaction.

'I think,' he said firmly, 'that you're drunk.'

'You don't think I'm pretty,' she mourned, blinking at him. 'I'm too thin, aren't I? First I was too fat and now I'm too thin.'

'I'm beside myself with lust,' he said drily, not entirely untruthfully. 'Arms up.'

She looked at him. How lovely he was! She wanted him to hold her again, to make her feel safe. He didn't usually make her feel safe, quite the opposite, but tonight he didn't seem threatening. He was soft and gentle and when he touched her he made her feel wanted, made the woman part of her fill with an aching longing.

'Francesca,' he said thickly, as he watched her eyes becoming heavy-lidded with unspoken desire, 'if you don't let me put this nightdress on you something is going to happen that we'll both regret tomorrow.'

'I won't regret it,' she said sulkily. How could she regret being loved? She put her hand out and touched him on the chest, sliding inside the damp towelling to find the powerful thud of his heart.

'You might not, but I would,' he murmured, his hand gently shackling her wrist as he removed her hand. 'I refuse to be seduced by brandy and shock.' He kissed her hand and smiled with wry self-derision. 'Perhaps if it was one or the other, but not both! Ask me again in the morning when you're in full possession of all your senses and I'll be delighted to respond.'

While she absorbed his rejection he wrestled her, with some difficulty, into her gown and robe, roughly tightening the belt as if it would provide more than a flimsy protection against their desires, should they get out of hand.

'A pity you weren't always so scr—scrup——' she hiccuped and abandoned the elusive word, '—didn't always have such scruples.'

'What do you mean?' He cupped her head with one hand while he rubbed her hair with a towel, then combed his fingers through the damp curls.

'You were quite happy to seduce an innocent——' the word tangled on her tongue, '—girl for a bet.'

His hands stilled in her hair, then slowly lowered to tilt her flushed face to his. 'You *knew* about that?'

His shock briefly penetrated her protective haze. Oops, she hadn't meant to tell him that. 'Knew about what?' she asked with what she thought was extreme cunning, unaware that her eyes were grey with guilty knowledge. Ross sighed and reached back for the half-empty brandy glass he had put on the coffee table. He held it to her lips, which she pressed together with a lop-sided frown.

'Are you trying to get me drunk?'

'You're already drunk, Princess. A little more isn't going to make much difference.' But it might loosen her unwary tongue.

It sounded supremely logical. 'I've never had a hangover before,' she confided proudly and wondered why his mouth tugged down at the corners in that funny, kind of sad way as she sipped. Tenderly he fed her the rest of the glass and between sips softly kissed and coaxed her into rambling honesty. He was behaving like an unprincipled bastard, but dammit, he *needed* to know.

When she told him, half-way between a giggle and a sob, that she had overheard the settling-up of his bet about their date that fateful Monday morning in the bike shed, he groaned and closed his eyes, tilting his lovely shaggy head back. 'Oh, God...'

When he looked at her again, nestled against his side, his eyes were deep blue with regret. 'I'm sorry, Fran, but if you heard everything, surely——'

'I didn't stay to hear *all* the gory details,' she interrupted him with a tipsy attempt at haughty dignity. She had rushed away and hidden in the girls' toilet, feeling ugly and soiled and utterly humiliated.

A few more sips and she let it all spill out... how she had been too shy to actively seek him out in the school grounds, but had hovered near the bike sheds where the boys gathered, hoping to 'accidentally' run into him and defy her grandparents' strictures by cementing the friendship that he had proposed on Saturday night.

'Did you get her blouse open? I'm not paying up on this bet until you give us the brand of her bra. I bet it was an armoured one, with a royal crest on it: Princess Pudge.' The snickering adolescent voice had hit Francesca like a blow.

'I guess you really earned your dough, huh, Ross? We should have offered you danger money on top of the bet... you could have been suffocated just *trying* to find first base, let alone touching it!'

Francesca hadn't waited for the raucous young laughter to die so that she could hear Ross besmirch the lovely memory of their hours together. Princess Pudge! The tender shoots of womanhood had shrivelled before the vision of him parading her loving vulnerability for his friends to paw over and laugh at. Later, when Ross had asked her to sit with him at lunch, she had lashed out at him with all her pain, grinding his pride into the dust as he had hers.

'Ah, Princess, if only I'd known,' Ross sighed, rocking her gently in his arms, finally solving the puzzle of how the shyly passionate girl who had touched his arrogant young heart had turned into the cool, disdainful princess his wounded ego demanded he dislike and avoid. 'No wonder you attacked me with those painful truths...you must have hated me...'

Fran twisted her head to peer up at him, wondering why he was suddenly receding like that, going furry around the edges. And he looked so serious, so regretful. She wanted to make him smile, make him feel all warm and deliciously woozy, the way she felt...

'Don' hate you, Ross...' Her tongue got tangled up as she tried to screw her eyes into focus, 'Only you...' Her words sank into a drowsy slur, '...was lies, 'nyway. No boys...' She smiled dreamily. 'Only you...'

'Francesca? What do you mean, lies? Francesca, wake up!' Ross looked in exasperation at the sleeping woman curled so trustingly in his arms. He didn't have the heart to wake her up; their unfinished business would have to be settled in the morning. His mouth curved wryly. In the morning she would be bolting for her high horse again, and he welcomed the notion of being there when she found the stable empty!

CHAPTER SIX

'FRANCESCA, wake up!'

Francesca surfaced reluctantly, a suffering husk of nauseous vibrations. She groaned as sunlight pierced her aching eyeballs. The act of lifting her head prompted an excruciating pain in her skull that screamed for relief. Her mouth tasted so vile that every time she swallowed her stomach tightened ominously. She groaned again, softly, as she became aware of someone perching on the edge of her bed, causing dangerous fluctuations in the mattress.

'Go 'way,' she slurred, wanting to be left alone in her misery.

'I've brought you some coffee, and this...' The monster of callousness waved a plate with a piece of thin, scarcely buttered toast on it, across her bleary vision.

'Oh, God——' She clapped a hand to her mouth.

Ross grinned an offensively healthy grin and put the coffee and plate down on the chair beside her bed. He hauled her protesting body up against her pillow and held her there with one large hand braced on her shoulder.

'Part of the problem is that you haven't eaten any-thing for nearly twenty-four hours—it's nearly eleven am, you know—and you're probably suffering a bit of dehy-dration as well. Come on, it's only weak, but it's liquid.'

He held up the coffee cup to her lips and tilted it so that she had to sip, or have it poured down the neck of her nightdress. It hit her stomach, warm and wet, but

98

before she could moan again a piece of toast was inserted into her unwary mouth.

'Nibble.'

Fran chewed and swallowed cautiously. This time when Ross put the cup to her lips she removed it from his hand and drank. He watched approvingly, his blue eyes clear and sparkling with life, his skin smooth-shaven and glossy, his chestnut hair combed damply into unaccustomed style. Fran closed her eyes to shut out the vision of physical well-being, grateful and annoyed to find his simple remedy working. She felt marginally better.

'You got me drunk,' she accused.

'*You* got drunk, I only provided the bottle.'

Fran opened her eyes with a suddenness that hurt. 'I distinctly remember——' she began as aggressively as her condition would allow. Then she distinctly remembered...

'What?' Ross looked interested, his mouth a give-away straight line as he watched her face change from a sickly shade of green to a delicate rose.

'Nothing.' She buried her nose hurriedly in her cup.

'Nothing? You mean, you don't remember.'

She scowled. 'I remember what we *didn't* do.'

'Only because I was too much of a gentleman to take advantage of your kind offer,' he said smugly.

'*You*, a gentleman!' Her snicker hurt the back of her eyes and she rested her head momentarily on her shoulder, unaware that the hunching movement made her neckline dip alarmingly, enticingly.

'Darling,' came the purring answer, 'you batted your eyelashes at me, and draped and nestled and nudged like a little kitten wanting to be petted. And *I* said, ask me again in the morning. Are you going to follow through, Princess, and bless me with your royal favours?'

'Go to hell,' she snarled wretchedly, not wanting to dwell on her brandy-induced wantonness of the night before. He was taking shameless advantage of her hangover and if she weren't so weak she would make him regret it.

'I can't do that, I'm afraid, Frankie. Not until we've finished our little talk. You passed out on me last night just as things were getting interesting.'

Fran's stomach somersaulted. Her memory was fragmentary, but she had a sinking feeling she had really let it all hang out. 'Please, can't we leave it until later? I'm really feeling pretty rotten.' She nibbled forlornly on another triangle of toast, making her eyes as big and as shamelessly mournful as she could manage.

He grinned. 'No dice, Frankie.' He folded his arms across his chest, swivelling sideways on the bed so that he loomed over her shrinking figure. 'You were saying something about lying about the boys...about there being only me. Were you, by any chance, referring to those classy dates of yours that you compared me so unfavourably with?'

He waited patiently until she had finished all the toast and let her fiddle with her coffee cup for a long minute before he demonstrated his determination. 'Francesca,' he said silkily, 'shall I fetch the brandy?'

The very thought made her pale.

'You're not in the best physical condition at the moment and it wouldn't take much effort to hold you down while I pour the stuff down your throat,' he said with cruel relish. 'When you're drunk you're very suggestible, and it doesn't seem to take much to turn you on your ear. In fact, I think I like you tipsy, Princess, falling all over me, trying to pull off my clothes...'

'I didn't!'

He grinned at her, and took the cup from her nerveless fingers.

'Beast,' she protested half-heartedly as he bent to put the cup on the floor.

His grin faded. 'Frankie, it started out as a bet, but I really liked you...'

'Sure. Look, Ross, it was a long time ago, I don't see that it needs dragging up again. For God's sake, we were children!' she burst out. Humiliations, like fears, were best forgotten.

'*You* were a child. I was everything you accused me of being,' he astounded her by saying. 'An arrogant young punk without the guts to apologise for doing something that I knew was wrong.'

Was her hangover causing her brain to mistranslate what her ears were hearing? Francesca stared at his expression of wry self-derision, slightly open-mouthed, and highly suspicious of his motives.

Ross lent over and gently pushed her lower jaw closed. 'I'm telling you this because then we can wipe the slate clean of any old grievances that might be cluttering up our subconscious. If only you had thrown that bet in my face at the time, or if you had hung around the bike shed a bit longer: I paid up, Frankie.'

'You...?'

'I paid up.'

She believed him. Why did she believe him? Francesca was shaken by the tiny bud of delight in her breast. What on earth did it matter, after all this time? But it did, and she was acutely conscious of it as Ross continued his wry confession.

'I told the guys that I had lost the bet. That you'd come out with me, but that you'd refused to fool around. They gave me hell, but I thought it was worth it. I liked you. Why do you think that no one taunted you about it? Because I'd threatened to punch the lights out of any guy who breathed a word outside the gang...they thought it was because I didn't want anyone to know how much I'd bombed out, but it was really because I didn't want it to get in the way of our friendship... not until I'd confessed to you, although I do admit there was a large chunk of ego involved, too.' He looked at her surprise-softened grey-blue eyes and his mouth pulled down. 'Then, when you gave me that haughty put-down in front of them all and I thought that you were just a clever tease who had gone slumming for a night, I wished like hell that I hadn't made the big sacrifice, but I couldn't recant without looking more of a fool than I already did. So I pretended that I didn't care.'

'I...you did a good job,' said Francesca shakily. When he had shrugged off her insults that day she had thought it merely confirmed his shallowness. In the intensity of her hurt she had never permitted him a point of view. As far as she was concerned, he hadn't deserved one.

'So did you,' he said with a pointed smile. 'On that date you were so serious to begin with, and so shy, and then you began to open up and I had flattered myself it was because of me. And when I touched you, you were so warm and soft and shyly generous that *I* was touched, macho jerk that I was. You came across as innocent and yet quietly mature, and so different from the general run of girls that I dated that I felt ashamed of what I had set out to do... see how far I could go with you just for the sake of impressing a bunch of guys. I realised that it was demeaning to both of us. I wanted to stand up to your grandfather for you, but you wouldn't let me and that made me feel even worse. And then, when Monday came around, I felt incredibly betrayed—hoist with my own petard. I couldn't stomach the thought that you were laughing up your sleeve at this crude jerk who had actually presumed that you'd want to get to know him better.'

'And I thought that you and your friends were all laughing behind my back at me,' said Fran ruefully, remembering the adolescent misery of that last term with an almost affectionate nostalgia.

'I never meant to hurt you, Frankie. I guess I got my just desserts.' He smoothed a curl back from her flushed cheek. 'I had some brutal thoughts about teaching you the dangers of putting on that act of sexy, eager innocence with guys with no claim to class. But it wasn't an act, was it, Frankie?'

'I——' She knew that his belated honesty begged honesty in return, but she was beginning to panic, wondering where all this was going to lead.

'There weren't any other boys, were there? Classier or otherwise. No sneaking out from boarding school?'

Francesca shrugged and picked at her nails to avoid his gaze, mumbling her reply into the neckline of her gown.

'What?' Ross ducked his head closer and she caught the spicy-clean male scent of him. It had almost the same effect as brandy. She jerked her head back against the pillows to try and preserve her ragged composure.

'I said no,' she muttered grudgingly.

'That was just wounded pride talking?'

'Yes.' She sighed. it was ridiculous to feel resentful after he had just delivered such a handsome apology.

'And you didn't really find me crude and clumsy, that was pride, too, mmm?' He was walking two fingers up her arm and Fran watched them approach the vulnerable scoop of her bare collarbone with bated breath.

'I...I suppose...'

'What do you suppose?' he asked, finding her warm, rapid pulse with one finger while the other stroked the fine soft skin of her throat. 'Did you mean it last night when you said there was only me? Was I the first boy to touch you? Was *I* the one who taught you how to french kiss?'

He watched the colour flow up under his fingers and his eyes deepened to a potent azure as he studied her blush. 'You're not still shy, are you, Frankie? I may have been the first, but I wasn't the last, was I?'

Her eyes flew open to deny him that arrogant satisfaction. 'Certainly not!' Though he wasn't going to force her to admit that he had been the yardstick beside which she had measured physical attraction ever since...and no one, not even the man she had eventually gone to bed with, had aroused her as strongly and easily as Ross did...*had*! 'You didn't blight my life, you know, Ross. I haven't been a languishing case of arrested virginity——'

'Waiting for Prince Charming to come along and re-awaken you,' he finished when she paused to wonder where that sentence was taking her.

'Precisely,' she said, brushing his unsettling touch away and adjusting the bedclothes primly across her breasts. 'I'm a normal, mature woman, quite comfortable with my...my...'

'Sexuality?' he supplied helpfully.

'Yes.' She glared at him and he laughed.

'Good. Then you're not going to get all uptight when I tell you that last night we slept together.'

'What?' Her shriek only made him laugh harder. Her blush deepened as she suddenly noticed the extra pillow that lay on the floor beside the bed. A vague remembrance stirred in the back of her mind, of a delicious warmth that she had clung to. Oh, God, had she actually let him...?

'When I tried to tuck you in you wouldn't let me. You kept saying that I was rocking the boat. You wouldn't quieten down until I got in beside you and anchored you in my arms.'

Francesca groaned and closed her eyes. 'We slept together?' Why couldn't she remember the details? She didn't imagine that making love with Ross Tarrant would be a forgettable experience. Perhaps he had been so fantastic that her mind was in a state of shock. Yes, that was far more likely!

'"Slept" being the operative word,' he said with a humorous gravity that jerked her eyes open. 'We were both too tired to do anything else. Besides——' his mouth indented wryly, '—the bed is a bit narrow to do much else...I like a bit of space when I exercise my desires, and my women willing, if not actually conscious...'

Fran opened her mouth to make a stinging reply, but closed it again when she realised that she had nothing to reproach him with. Whatever his motives, he *had* looked after her yesterday, in spite of their earlier row, and he hadn't taken advantage of her with anything other than words. *Worse luck*, whispered a voice from her heart which she drowned out by asking, 'How are you? Is your shoulder all right?'

He moved it experimentally. 'A little stiff. But stop trying to change the subject. I think your behaviour last night acknowledges an important truth, don't you?'

'Oh?' She looked at him warily. Was he going to accuse her of being a frustrated spinster...or a wanton?

'That it's still there.'

'W-what is?' she asked huskily, transfixed by the sapphire eyes.

'Whatever chemistry that was at work between us when we were too young to appreciate its potent rarity.'

'I...I don't know what you're talking about,' she denied hollowly.

'Frankie...' He shook his head in amused reproof, reading the feminine panic in the flickering grey eyes as an invitation to seduction. 'I considered myself pretty blasé at seventeen. I thought I knew it all...particularly where girls were concerned. You taught me differently. You taught me that sex is the greatest and most unknowable mystery of all...that it has as much to do with the mind as with the body. You can't force an attraction to someone, it's either there or it's not, and the chemistry is in the brain rather than the loins. You may see no rhyme nor reason for it, but it's there...as it is for us, as it was then, and now...'

And ever shall be the little voice echoed the prayer, *for ever and ever.*

'No...' She feebly denied the inevitable even as she lay there, watching his mouth approach, wanting yet afraid...

'Yes...' His teeth sank softly into her vulnerable lower lip, his certainty absorbed into the pores of her skin as he lowered himself on to the bed, pushing her back into the pillow, so that she accepted the weight of his chest against her tingling breasts, the fresh, clean scent of him in her nostrils, the taste of him in her mouth.

The intimate curl of his tongue inside her mouth set off a chain reaction in her body which recoiled even as it delighted in a trapped feeling of pleasure. *You can't escape*, she thought eagerly, *so you may as well enjoy it.*

As a hangover remedy it was without equal. The touch and taste of him sweetened every sense and sent a burst of adrenalin through her veins. It was like leaping that crevasse, all fear and a crazy sense of triumph at the challenge of the unkown...for, to Fran, this heated sexual urgency *was* largely unknown. It had been building inside since she had first seen Ross staring at her nakedness in the spa pool, a brooding, masculine threat...since long before that, since he had planted that dormant seed in a young girl's body, now germinating into the full flower of passion.

The kisses flowed like heady wine from mouth to mouth, and they were both breathing hard when he finally lifted his head and they stared at each other in crackling silence. He noticed with satisfaction the stormy glaze of the grey-blue eyes, the flush of arousal mantling the creamy skin of her face and throat, the provocative part of her slightly swollen mouth, while she was conscious of the full heaviness of his body as he lay on top of her, the hard, masculine pressure points imprinted on her as if he were the erotic template and she the silky bolt of cloth to be cut to fit his shape.

He kissed her again, a long, slow, thorough kiss, and then murmured against the corner of her mouth, 'If you're thinking what I'm thinking, Princess, I'm afraid we'll have to postpone. I don't think I could look my mother in the eye if she asked why we were late for lunch.'

Fran gasped. It was Sunday! She had forgotten about Jason's invitation.

'I wasn't thinking——'

He cut her off with another quick kiss. 'Yes, you were, and this time you can't blame the brandy.' He rolled off her and stood up beside the bed, looking down at her flushed confusion. 'Some time soon we're going to be lovers, Francesca, and finish what we started thirteen years ago...'

She gazed at his retreating back with a mixture of fascination and stunned anger. He made it sound so simple, like predestination. But Fran wasn't about to be seduced by fate. She tried to shake off the odd, empty ache in her body as she armoured herself in a carefully demure skirt and blouse. So what if there was a strong physical attraction between them? They weren't animals, they didn't *have* to give in to it just because it was there.

To her chagrin Ross chuckled when he saw her clothes.

'Who do you think that's going to fool, Princess? I know what sinful passions lurk beneath that starchy breast.'

'If you don't behave, I'm not coming,' she told him haughtily.

'Scout's honour.' He held up a hand, a pious look on the handsome face.

'You were never a Scout, Ross Tarrant,' she accused.

'Gigolo's honour, then.' He grinned at her disapproval.

'I don't believe that, either,' she sniffed as she marched out of the cabin.

'Took you long enough,' he said lazily as he handed her into the pick-up. 'Would you like to know what I really do for a living?'

'No.'

'Sure?' he teased knowingly, reading the frustrated curiosity in her stubborn profile. Now when she put on her prim and proper act it amused rather than annoyed him, because he knew it was only an act, that underneath she was feeling vulnerable.

'I'm not in the least interested,' she lied loftily, planning to dig the information out of his family over lunch, but casually, so he wouldn't realise what she was doing.

'Still, I think you ought to be prepared——'

'Are you going to start this thing, or do you want me to drive?'

'But, Fran——' He was laughing at her again, over some secret joke, and she had no intention of playing the straight woman to his punchline.

'Oh, go row a boat!' she snapped childishly.

'Shrew.' He clicked his tongue in tender exasperation as he started the car. 'OK, but it's your funeral, Princess. Don't get mad at me later.'

'Of course I won't.' Managing to imply that he wasn't worth getting upset over.

His hum filled the silence between them as the car wound along the inland road. Fran looked out the window to hide her smile. She didn't want to admit it to the smug man beside her, but she enjoyed bickering with him. She had never allowed herself the luxury of arguing with a man before, flexing her will against his; she had always been too shy, too uncertain of herself as a woman. If she hadn't liked or agreed with what a man said, she had simply withdrawn and naturally, she realised with hindsight, that had set limits on every relationship she had entered. Not even Brian had known what she really thought or felt, so she couldn't really blame him for his furious reaction when the cumulation of years of frustration had exploded on his head.

With Ross it was different. From the very first his boldness had made her bold. Because he had expected the worst from her, and she from him, she had felt free to let her feelings rip. And the unspoken physical attraction that had run concurrent with the surface animosity had spiced her reactions with a delicious exhilaration. But what would happen now, now that the unspoken was voiced? Where did they go from here? Where did she *want* to go?

Lunch with the Tarrants proved to be a small series of revelations, capped off by an enormously shattering one.

First surprise was the warmth with which Florence Tarrant welcomed Fran into the big, sunny kitchen of the large, rambling old house. After scolding her son for his tardiness in not bringing Francesca along before, she simply opened her arms and hugged the young woman as if she was a long-lost relative.

'You're looking as if a puff of wind would blow you away. I hope Ross is looking after you. I'm so sorry about Ian, my dear. It must make you feel very alone now.'

Fran felt a prickle of unexpected tears at the back of her throat and swallowed hastily. The casually affectionate embrace touched a deep chord within her. Such gestures had been few and far between in her past. Physical affection from her grandparents had been rationed so that she wouldn't be 'spoiled', and she had no memories of her own mother, who had rejoined her roving lover when Fran was only four months old and been killed with him in a car accident two years later.

'It does a bit,' she admitted to the slim, dark-haired older woman, surprised at the impulse to confide to an almost total stranger. 'Which is a bit hypocritical, I suppose, since we saw each other so little, and didn't get on very well when we did get together.'

'Not silly at all.' Florence Tarrant smiled in warm understanding. 'We all tend to take certain basics in our life for granted, like family ties, until suddenly they're not there any more.' The soft brown eyes began to twinkle as she looked from Fran to her son. 'You'll just have to create some blood ties of your very own to take for granted.'

It took Fran a moment to realise what she meant. When she did she blushed to the roots of her hair and sent Ross a speaking look when he laughed at her stam-

mering attempts to explain that there was nothing between them.

'If you say so, my dear,' Florence Tarrant said, with
a placid smile that was both sympathetic and
disbelieving.

'I told you she was trying to marry me off,' Ross
whispered in her ear as they went into the large, wood-
panelled dining-room.

'I can understand her desperation!' Fran shot back.
'Ageing playboys must have a pretty limited value on
the glutted marriage market.'

Ross got his revenge for that remark when they were
seated and Fran had been introduced to a bewildering
array of people: Beth, a sweetly feminine version of Ross
with long, straight dark hair and flashing blue eyes, and
her morose-looking boyfriend, John, who seemed glumly
aware he wasn't going to hold this young butterfly's attention for long; Ross's youngest brother, David, who
worked with Jason in the family business and, except
for his husky size, took after his mother with his dark
hair and eyes, and the three, leather-jacketed and vaguely
menacing members of his band, Mo, Bean and Adam;
the patriarch, Mike Tarrant, as broad-shouldered as his
three sons and looking amazingly fit for a man in his
mid-sixties, his blue eyes alert and his gruff voice offset
by the same world-embracing friendliness that his wife
possessed. Jason and Tessa, to Francesca's left on the
long, polished wood table, were welcome, familiar faces,
but she wasn't given a chance to say more than hello
before Ross made his dramatic announcement.

'Sorry we were late, folks, but you can thank Francesca that I'm sitting here at all. She saved my life
yesterday.'

'Saved your life? Wow!' Beth's lovely eyes widened
with awe. 'What happened?'

Stricken with embarrassment at being the centre of attention, Fran could only stare daggers at Ross, lounging cheerfully at her right elbow. She had thought he would have kept silent about his ignominious expedition, but it seemed that he was happy to court his family's disfavour for the sake of embarrassing her.

Grinning back at her, he launched into a colourful, graphic description of the previous day's rescue, drawing a clamour of admiration for the blushing heroine.

'He wasn't really in any danger——' she tried to say, but her attempted modesty was brushed aside as Ross came in for his share of derision.

'I would have tipped him out of the thing and made *him* swim back, 'David crowed cockily over his brother's ignominy. Two years younger than Jason, he obviously grabbed every opportunity he could to repay years of teasing by his two impressive elder brothers.

'I wouldn't have blamed you, Francesca, if you'd left him to the coastguard,' his mother said with amazing placidity. 'They would have given him a good talking to. I hope you have no ill effects from your heroics, my dear.'

'Only a hangover,' put in Ross wickedly, but this time Fran refused to blush. He had actually done her a favour, in an embarrassing way. He had ensured her instant acceptance by his family. Or is that what he had intended? She looked at him uncertainly, and he winked.

'He plied me with brandy afterwards,' she said, deciding to twist his mockery to her own advantage. 'So I guess the hangover is his fault too!' She shrugged with an air of injured innocence.

'Ross!' His mother's reproach was all that she could have wished for.

'Medicinal purposes only, Mum,' said Ross defensively. 'She was in shock. I think she realised what an unnecessary risk she had taken.'

'Unnecessary risk? *I* took?' Encouraged by the empathetic vibrations from around the table, Fran took umbrage. '*You're* the dumb ox who thinks that risks are only there to be taken. *You're* the one who rowed off in a childish huff just because I wouldn't lie down and let you wipe your arrogant feet all over me! *You're* the one who started the whole argument by trying to get rid of me by domestic violence.'

'He hits you?' sqawked Beth, looking at her brother with new eyes, and to Fran's surprise and amusement Ross actually blushed.

'Of course I don't hit her,' he growled. 'That's not to say she couldn't do with a damned good spanking on occasion.'

'Ross!' Florence Tarrant metaphorically rapped his knuckles.

'That's a pretty sexist remark to make. I'm surprised at you, Ross,' Tessa put in her quiet voice. Her face was serious, but when she flicked a glance at Francesca her eyes were filled with the same amusement reflected in her fiancé's. Francesca grinned back.

'I didn't mean physical violence,' she explained sweetly. 'I meant his horrific lack of willingness to lift a finger around the house. He's as domesticated as a wild boar.

'But I taught all my sons domestic chores,' Mrs Tarrant protested, 'Ross, what have you been doing to poor Francesca?'

'What indeed?' murmured Ross, humour twitching at his mouth again as he met Francesca's demure gaze. 'Stirrer,' he muttered, for her ears only.

'I must admit that he does more than his share of the cooking, though,' she said quickly, conscious of the threat of the long, hard thigh suddenly pressed against hers. She shifted her legs. He followed, tangling his feet with hers. Above the table their eyes duelled. 'He's a great cook, but he's useless anywhere else but the kitchen.'

'Oh, really?' Jason gave a shout of laughter. 'Poor Ross. Bedside manner slipping, is it, doctor?'

'Now, Jason,' his mother admonished him mildly.

'Sorry, Francesca,' Jason's apology was unabashed. 'It's just that you must be the first nurse Ross has ever met who hasn't instantly succumbed to the great healer's charm. Told you it was just the white coat, Ross.'

Fran's slightly bewildered smile froze on her lips. She felt Ross's hand come down warningly on her knee.

'You should have let me explain when I wanted to, Princess,' he breathed in a singsong manner out of the corner of his mouth.

Her puzzlement, however, was misinterpreted by everyone else. 'I can see by your blank expression that you haven't worked at National Women's Hospital, Francesca,' Beth giggled. 'After the Dream Consultant has made his rounds there they have to sweep 'em up from the hallways...swooning nurses and patients alike!'

Consultant? Doctor? Ross was a *doctor*?

Fran's head swivelled stiffly to her right. The deep azure eyes were filled with rueful apology, and an unholy amusement that was almost her undoing.

He was a doctor! Ross...that lazy, teenage intellectual sloven, had trained to be a *doctor*! When? How? She went icy with embarrassment when she recalled some of the things she had said to him, and then sizzled hot with fury. How he must have enjoyed watching her make an arrant fool of herself! The only redeeming feature of his wretched joke was that he didn't appear to have told anyone else of her misconception...the misconception he had deliberately fostered!

CHAPTER SEVEN

'FRANCESCA?' She came out of her fierce trance to meet Mrs Tarrant's concern. 'Are you all right? You've gone quite pale. Ross, perhaps you should have kept her in bed.'

'I tried, believe me, Mum, I tried.' Ross's smirk sent the colour flooding back into Francesca's face. She placed her hand on his under the table and dug in her nails. He jerked back in his seat with a strangled cough. Nursing his branded hand in his lap, he had the gall to send Fran a reproachful look. 'I ... er ... think she's recovered now. Perhaps it was a momentary swoon ...'

'It takes more than just a pretty face to set Auckland Hospital nurses swooning.' Francesca gave him a sweet, murderous smile.

'No, it takes a good slug or two of brandy to do that,' Ross agreed, equally sweetly.

Francesca wanted to sink through the floor. Even the ravenous, leather-jacketed trio at the other end of the table stopped eating their way through third helpings in order to follow the intriguing conversation.

'Now, Frankie, you said you wouldn't get mad,' Ross teased, his eyes glinting with provocative triumph, knowing that she could say little without revealing what a gullible idiot she had been. Why hadn't she suspected? The way he'd talked about his injuries, the intelligent questions he had asked when she'd talked about her work—they should have given her clues. But she had been blinded by other things, not the least of which had been the instant, unwelcome attraction she had felt for him.

He was enjoying this, damn him, and she could tell from his disgustingly smug expression that he thought that just because he had now proved how utterly respectable he was that everything would go his way...that she would fall gratefully into his manly arms!

She managed a creditable laugh. 'I'm not mad. I was just thinking that whatever we do we seem to end up diametrically opposed.' She dazzled Ross with a brilliant smile that made the amused blue eyes narrow with suspicion. Brace yourself, *Doctor*, Fran thought with grim satisfaction, one good bombshell deserves another! 'Here you are, local boy made good...a doctor, no less, and here *I* am, always the goody-two-shoes at school, going sadly to the dogs, according to my friends.'

She savoured the laughing protests and enquiries, not taking her eyes off the still and silent Ross, seeing his suspicion harden into scepticism. He thought she was just coat-trailing.

'But you're a nurse. That's as good as a doctor in my book!' Beth was saying. 'Ross says that nurses are the backbone of the Health Service.'

'They are. But I'm not a nurse any more.'

Ross didn't change colour and not a muscle moved in his face, but the sheer blue shock of his eyes was worth the price of baring her life to a bunch of virtual strangers. Francesca raised her eyebrows mockingly.

'Shall I loosen your collar, Doctor? Some hot, sweet tea, perhaps?' A brief storm darkened the blue eyes and she grinned delightedly, a wicked mischief dancing across her wide mouth. And he thought that *he* had the monopoly on provocation!

'My dear.' Florence Tarrant tugged her attention away from her helpless victim so that Francesca didn't see the storm clear as swiftly as it had come, to be replaced by a sultry gleam of admiration, and a determination which would have disturbed her greatly had she seen it. 'Surely you haven't had to give up your career permanently because of your illness? After all your training!'

'Oh, no,' Francesca told her hostess, touched by her evident sympathy, and guilty because she didn't really deserve it. 'I resigned just before I came up here, but I never actually intended nursing to be a life-long vocation when I started out. It was as much a way to escape home as a desire to help people.' Florence Tarrant smiled understandingly, without a hint of the disapproval that Fran had faced from others about 'wasting her training', and she was encouraged to expand. 'I've enjoyed myself, and learned a lot but . . . well . . . now I have a chance to do what I always wanted. I'm going into business with a friend.'

'Really? What kind of business?'

'Gardening.' Fran flushed slightly at the soft, incredulous sound from the man beside her. She kept her gaze firmly fixed on Florence Tarrant's surprised interest. 'My grandmother said it wasn't any kind of job for a well brought-up young lady, and I wasn't very assertive back in those days so I chose second-best. But I've kept up gardening as a hobby and taken several extensive courses on horticulture. Since I've become a qualified nurseryman——'

'Nursery*person*,' corrected Tessa with a grin which Fran returned in brief.

'—my friend Christina—who runs a plant shop—and I have been making plans to expand her shop into a garden centre as a base for a contract-gardening business. We were having trouble with our bank loan and probably would have had to postpone for another few years until...well...when Grandfather died I realised that our problems were solved.'

'One door closing, another opening.' Mrs Tarrant eased Francesca's fear that they would think her mercenary. 'I wish you the best of luck, Francesca, it'll be a great adventure. I'm a keen gardener, too, but I'm not terribly knowledgeable. Perhaps you'd like to give me some advice...I've got some stubborn spots where nothing seems to grow...'

Ross settled back in his chair, turning his powerful body in Fran's direction as she ignited to his mother's interest.

So...Francesca wasn't going to invest her unexpected windfall in blue-chip stock or a nice, safe, retirement fund. She was going to risk it on the roll of a die! For, in the current economic climate, anyone starting up a small business, even one with solid financial backing, was taking a gamble.

How she had enjoyed throwing it in his face. Ross looked down at the fast-fading indentations in the back of his hand and smiled inwardly. At least her tit-for-tat revelation had defused her anger at his own. She could hardly start throwing stones in his direction now. He lifted his eyes to her animated profile, amused by her determination to ignore him, but content to study her at leisure as she chatted with his mother. Some of that bright confidence was bravado, he realised...typically Fran. She was such a mixture of fierce independence and sweet vulnerability, bravery and cowardice, that it wasn't surprising that she had confused him at times. In all probability she confused herself even more. She would never admit it, of course, but Fran was starved for praise, for approval...for love...it showed in the way that she flowered shyly under the slightest sign of interest, and the startled pleasure she took in the easy acceptance of his family. And yet a veneer of protective caution prevented her from reaching out, from trusting that she wouldn't be rebuffed. It was typical that even in making this quantum leap into an unknown future she was still following some immutable plan, her eyes fixed firmly on her goal, allowing for no deviation from her set course.

Ross intended to show her some interesting detours, only slightly concerned that he had no particular destination in mind, only a series of intriguing signposts to follow. He wasn't sure when she had stopped being merely an intellectual and sexual challenge—and he was never one to resist *that*! If the compulsion to have her had been merely physical he could have done so by now, he had that much confidence in the mutuality of the attraction, but the complex shadings of her deceptive personality had added a completely unpredictable element to his desire.

Francesca, becoming increasingly uncomfortable at the silent, heavy-lidded stare she could feel from the man next to her, was grateful for Mrs Tarrant's suggestion of a tour of her gardens. But she couldn't escape Ross for long. He came out to tell his mother that she was wanted on the telephone, then stood, barring Francesca's way through a vine-covered arch between the barn and double garage.

'Are we quits, Frankie?' he asked softly, tilting his head to one side so that the sun gilded his hair and the smooth, hard line of his jaw.

Fran stiffened her shoulders. 'I suppose you thought it great fun to pretend to be some out-of-work hobo. You must have really laughed when I worried about your health!'

'Actually, it annoyed the hell out of me,' he said wryly. 'I'm afraid I was too busy trying to strut my macho stuff to thank you at the time. Thanks for caring, Fran.'

'I didn't care,' she denied with a sniff. 'I would have been the same whoever you were. It was nothing personal.'

'Does your impersonal concern always lead to your seducing your patients?' he enquired with interest, and to her fury she blushed.

'You...you...you...' She sought for an adequate description.

'*Doctor!*' spat out Ross in such tones of loathing that Fran felt a traitorous frisson of laughter shiver up her spine. 'Somehow it doesn't sound as insulting as gigolo, does it?' he asked coaxingly.

'Ross——' Her voice trembled on the edge of a laugh. How dared he make her laugh when she wanted to be furious with him!

'Ah, Fran, stop trying to pretend that you're a prig. I think we've disproved that one entirely, haven't we? No woman with such passionate responses as yours could be a prig. I think your affinity with plants and nature is your basic earthiness seeking an outlet...'

Passionate? Earthy? Fran stared at him blankly. Neither she nor anyone else thought of her in those terms. Practical, disciplined, *com*passionate, yes...except in Ross's presence—then all those neatly dove-tailing pieces of her personality tended to break apart and float dizzily away. Each time she had more and more difficulty fitting them back together again. While she pondered the disquieting mental image, Ross moved closer until she became aware of the sun reflecting off his soft white linen shirt, warming the skin of her face. His blue eyes, like twin seas, beckoned her into deep waters.

'Let's face it, Frankie,' he said softly. 'It was you, not me, who was so anxious to preserve your misconceptions... I just went along for the ride. I'll admit that, at first, I thought you deserved the come-uppance, but that was before I realised *why* it was so important for you to think that I was an uncouth, muscle-bound, immoral reptile. It was both a defence and a weapon. You were afraid of your feelings for me. You were attracted to me, but you didn't want to commit yourself to that attraction. You felt safe wrapped in your moral outrage, because it meant that you could experience the vicarious sexual thrill of being with me without risking the emotional involvement that intimacy inevitably brings. In short, Princess, you were running scared.'

'Why, you conceited moron!' Fran was appalled at the accuracy of his guess. For the first time she wondered what kind of doctor he was. Was he, God forbid, a psychiatrist? Used to probing for motives and meanings? 'Is that a pompous way of accusing me of being a tease?'

She was horrified the moment the words popped out. She hadn't meant to say that. Hurriedly, she tried to recover. 'I mean, do you assume that every woman you meet is wildly attracted to you? That's one way of turning a rejection into an ego booster, I suppose.'

He ignored her jeer, choosing to answer the involuntary cry that she had revealingly blurted out. 'A tease is a woman who deliberately arouses a man just for the pleasure of slapping him down.' He moved suddenly and Fran flinched, but he was only stretching out his arms to lace his fingers through the woven wire of the archway in an attitude of unthreatening openness. Fran's restless desire to escape this disturbing discussion evaporated. As long as he didn't touch her she could handle the situation. Of course, there were other ways of touching.

Having Ross's tapering masculinity spreadeagled in front of her was like a caress to the senses. It presented a tempting illusion that Ross was offering himself to her, making himself vulnerable, the male as victim.

'I think that for the most part you don't realise what the hell you're doing, it's just pure instinct. But, Fran, sometimes you make me ache...'

'Then why didn't you——?' She bit her lip, but it was too late, the question was asked.

'Last night?' He understood her so well, too well... 'Because that's not the way I want it. I don't want to just relieve an ache in my groin, Frankie. I think that's what makes you so scared, mmm?'

She looked away from the warm blue invitation. 'I think *you're* the tease, Ross Tarrant...' she said shakily.

'I would never slap you down, honey, don't ever be afraid of that. Ever since I was seventeen I've had intermittent dreams about you, sometimes so vivid that it was as if I was actually touching and tasting you, the sweet, wild scent of you perfuming my lonely sheets...'

'Lonely!' Fran had to stop that erotic imagery. 'I doubt your bed is ever empty, let alone lonely. You know too much about women for your own good.'

He laughed. 'That's your fault, Princess.'

'Mine?'

'I have you to thank for what I am today.' His laughter faded into a wry seriousness at her puzzlement. 'What you said to that arrogant young punk took, Frankie. Initially it was my pride that drove me to try and prove you wrong about me, to take the hardest option there was. I didn't have bursary, but I went to university the next year. I was going for Bachelor of Science, but I did so well the first year that I switched to Medicine. It *wasn't* easy. As you so succinctly told me, I'd been lazy; I had to learn to discipline myself all over again——' he grinned at the memory. 'I didn't even have time to play sport. And then, when it came to specialising, I again used you for inspiration.'

'Oh?' Fran could tell by the glint in his eye that she needed to brace herself.

'Mmm . . . my natural talent, remember? My skill with women? I didn't lie to you about that, Frankie, they do pay to come and see me. I'm in great demand . . . as an obstetrician. Do you know, darling, that you look like a fish?'

Fran snapped her mouth shut. Suddenly it all made sense . . . the wicked way he had misled her by telling her *almost* the truth. She closed her eyes against that teasing grin. 'You . . . *wretch*!' Against her will she was laughing, and he was watching with a peculiar smile of satisfaction.

'I must say I was slightly miffed that you hadn't known, perhaps that's why I let you wander so far up the garden path,' he admitted when her laughter faded to adorable giggles that made her look like that shy teenager again. 'I had flattered myself that I was fairly well known in the medical fraternity . . . I'm in private practice, but I'm a consultant at National Women's, too.'

'Well, hospitals do tend to be rather insular,' Fran offered with a trace of apology. 'We get absorbed in our own little microcosm of wards and shifts, and I haven't been on an obstetric ward for years. I . . . can't believe it . . .' She stared at him and he could see from her face that she was threatening to go off into giggles again.

'Don't apologise, Fran,' he said drily. 'You don't want to break your record of consistently deflating my ego . . . although, thank God, there's one area in which you never fail to respond but flatteringly.'

The giggle froze in her throat, as he had meant it to. They stared at each other. Vine shadows laced the handsome face, sending ripples of darkness across the unruffled blue calm of his eyes. He hadn't moved, arms still outstretched, only the white tension-lines where his fingers gripped the wire revealing the control he was exercising. It would have been easy to take her into his arms and convince her that what he wanted she wanted also... but with Fran the easy option wasn't an option at all. Her submission had to be voluntary or it was valueless to both of them. The tightly wrapped petals protecting the feminine core of her personality couldn't be forced open... they would respond only to warmth and light and the promise of life-giving nourishment. Surely the Fran that he had learned about this afternoon could be coaxed to take the inevitable gamble that was involved in any human relationship...

'Why didn't you tell me what you wanted to do with the money, Fran?' He chose to take the oblique route.

The soft lilt in his voice as much as the abrupt change of subject disconcerted her. 'I... it was none of your business,' she said huskily.

'And now it is?' He deftly manipulated her answer. 'Have you decided that you don't need excuses any more?'

'Excuses?'

'To stay. You can't still believe that I'm after your inheritance any more... I never put in a formal claim anyway. So if you stay now, it's for one reason. You want to.'

Predictably, when cornered, Francesca panicked, looking for the exits. 'You think, just because I know you're a doctor and not some... layabout——'

'Oh, no, we've already dealt with that one, Princess,' he told her with quiet, inexorable reason. 'The attraction we share has nothing to do with what we *are*. Your status or mine has nothing to do with it. And don't make the mistake of thinking that just because I'm a profes-

sional that I'm suddenly invested with emotional re-
spectability. Part of me will always be a hell-raiser, always
open to a challenge...I've learned to reconcile the
conflictions of my character...I think you're just starting
to. You can be a woman *and* run a business, Francesca.
They aren't mutually exclusive.'

'I don't know yet that I can run a business.' Under
stress she admitted something that previously she would
never have dreamed of admitting. 'I...I'll need all my
time and energy to find out. I'm so close now, I can't
afford——'

'Other commitments? Spending a few more days with
me isn't a commitment, Fran. Hell, I have enough re-
sponsibilities in my own professional life to ensure that
I evade them as much as I can in my private life.'

A more straightforward proposal of dishonourable
intentions Fran couldn't imagine and she felt strangely
reassured. In effect it was a promise to let her dictate
the terms of their relationship which, combined with the
powerful feeling of inevitability which he had engen-
dered this morning, proved unbearably tempting. But
there were cross-currents between them that tugged
dangerously at her senses. What if she stayed and, God
forbid, fell in love with him? Every cautious bone in her
body went brittle at the idea of trusting her happiness
to someone else.

'I...should go back to Auckland.' She was disgusted
to hear her tongue change *must* into *should*.

'Why?' He was leaning so close, hanging from tense
fingers, that she could feel his breath fluttering on her
lashes. 'You told us at lunch that your partner is doing
all the paperwork, and that you've had the plans drawn
up for weeks. In another few days Simpson will have
squared Ian's estate, unchallenged, and you can leave

with a full statement of your assets to show your bank manager. Stay until then, Princess...'

At what point had the snide insult become an endearment? Fran wondered as she put a hand flat on his chest to stop herself falling forward into the blue void of his eyes. His chest rose quick and hard against her hand, her fingers sliding through the patch of hair revealed by the opened neck of his shirt.

'I...I can't...' absently, concentrating on the vibrations under her fingertips.

'You can...' The words formed against her lips, his tongue stroking its velvety roughness against their parted warmth, then plunging inside with a suddenness that made her head reel. The muscles of his arms bulged as his hands clenched convulsively against the wire at the inward sway of her body against the open trap of his. The slender, capable hand on his chest slid up around the rigid column of his neck, pulling him down to her, her other hand curving around his hard waist, fingers reaching down to splay against the muscular jut of his buttocks. Ross gave a soft groan in her mouth and arched hungrily into her softness, the powerful thighs supporting the potent thrust of his hips. Fran responded just as hungrily, realising dimly that his refusal to put his arms around her was a deliberate enticement, a sexual challenge that was impossible to resist.

She pushed a thigh between his, and he caught and held it against the centre of his body, letting her feel the rigid proof of his arousal. Yet still he didn't put his arms around her. With a hot surge of mingled power and frustration Fran pushed her rounded breasts against his chest, crushing the taut peaks with a shudder of masochistic pleasure, her mouth widening beneath the silken search of his tongue. Both hands were now clinging to his waist, sliding up under the sweatshirt to find the damp, ridging muscles of his back. Suddenly he tore his mouth away.

'Stay.'

Francesca stared at him with storm-grey eyes, feeling the small tremors that rippled through the powerful male body. The handsome face was flushed, the sensuous mouth full, the blue-hot flame in his eyes both frightening and exciting her. She had never dreamed she could make a man look like that: pleasure-racked from the mere touching mouths and bodies. Hanging there against the wire, he looked as if he was being tortured and she supposed that in way, he was...and she was the torturer. Guiltily she stepped back, but he caught her at last, his fingers white with the marks of the wire, cupping her face, the strain of his gentleness evident in the husky grating of his voice.

'No...stay.' He laid a finger against her mouth and moved it back and forth against the swollen fullness. 'In your own time, Frankie. I won't rush you, I won't hurt you...' And he gathered her delicately into him, his kiss deep and soft and infinitely sensuous. There was none of the tension of moments before, but passion aplenty, smooth and swift-running, freed of the turmoil of Fran's mental resistance. They were so engrossed they didn't hear the tentative electronic tuning from the barn develop into a hard-driving rhythm. Fran was listening to an inner music, far more lyrical. The sound vibrating the timbers of the barn concealed other noises, however, and Fran was highly embarrassed when her eyes fluttered open and she saw Jason and Tessa, hand in hand behind Ross, regarding them with twin expressions of amusement.

'Ross——' She squirmed, trying to push him away.

'Don't get skittish on me now, Princess——' His voice was velvet with sensual threat.

'Unhand the lady, thou blackhearted villain!' Jason grinned, causing his brother to spin around, keeping firm hold of the woman in his arms. 'A gentleman would heed a maiden's protest.'

To Fran's further embarrassment Ross didn't let her go. He scooped her around in front of him, pulling her back against his chest and linking his arms under her breasts so that they presented a united front to his brother.

'Ah, but the lady doth protest too much, and any *man* worth his salt knows what *that* means!' The chauvinistic teasing made Fran struggle to break his implacable grip, but her struggles ceased abruptly as Ross bent his head to murmur throatily in her ear, 'You'd better stay put, Princess. If you move away from me now you're going to embarrass the hell out of both of us.' He eased his hips forward to show her why and Fran felt a slow, tingling blush sweep through her body as an unmistakable hardness was cradled in the cleft of her buttocks. His arms tightened briefly, increasing her breathlessness, before relaxing as he felt her lean obediently back against him.

'Isn't he terrible?' Tessa shook her head cheerfully, embarking on what was obviously a well established family game. 'I mean, women flock to his practice because he has this reputation for being empathetic as well as a damned good doctor. But it's all a sham. He only *pretends* to believe that women are real people with functioning brains as well as bodies, but underneath he harbours these savage sexist fantasies...'

'Thank God you two are going to be married soon!' Ross muffled his laughter in the warm brown curls on Francesca's head. 'My professional advice, Jase, is barefoot and pregnant. It's the only way to control that beady-eyed obsession with dethroning the naturally dominant partner...'

'But Ross, I thought you knew, men can't *get* pregnant,' Tess shot back. 'There has to be another way. Fran, you really must do something about this character masquerading as a doctor. He doesn't even know the facts of *life*, for heaven's sake.'

'You mean about women being the naturally dominant partners? I know, I know. He really is incredibly thick,' said Fran, entering into the fray, only to be thoroughly trounced when Ross made a tiny rocking movement against her and said in a low voice, for her ears alone,

'Why, thank you, darling, I'm glad you're impressed.'

She was so flustered she missed the next few moments of lightly insulting banter, and yet it was a confusion she enjoyed. Wrapped in his arms, Fran felt warm and secure and very much at home, wryly aware of how drastically her opinion of him had changed in the short time she had known him. She guessed that women would indeed flock to his practice. Ross was a trifle arrogant, it was true, but it was an arrogance born of confidence in himself and his abilities, and tempered by a lazy charm that was a natural outgrowth of his warm and loving upbringing. It would be a point of pride with him to be the best at what he did, and to treat the whole woman rather than just her condition. Fran had known, and disliked, obstetricians and gynaecologists who used aloofness and medical jargon as a subtle form of intimidation on their patients. But Ross, with his tolerance and humour, would put a woman at her ease, enable her to express her questions and fears about her treatment without being made to feel that she was imposing on a busy man's time. Ross would earn his patient's respect instead of demanding it by virtue of his position...

Fran jumped as a reverberating boom from the barn was followed by a high-pitched electronic whine. Jason winced and said something that was drowned out by another ear-shattering sequence of chords.

'What?' Ross raised his voice to a shout.

'I said,' Jason yelled, 'why don't you invite Tess and I over for a spa this evening in your quiet haven? We'll bring the food if you provide the booze. How about it?'

'Anything to escape the new wave of the future,' Tessa laughed, hands over her ears, nodding towards the barn.

'Perhaps we can make a few waves of our own,' Jason leered, and was teasingly slapped for his pains. 'Shall we bring togs, Fran, or have you both carried on your skinny-dipping tradition?'

'Togs, please,' said Fran primly, ignoring Ross's sensuous chuckle, although she had a suspicion that even if she wore a suit of armour, one look from those sexy blue eyes and she would be naked before him, body and soul!

CHAPTER EIGHT

'BEAUTIFUL, isn't she?'

Faintly amused by Jason's proud parental air, Francesca ran her hand along the stiffened fabric of the lower wing of the biplane and was dutifully admiring. 'Lovely. What is it?'

'Tiger Moth—it was Dad's first plane. These things used to be the backbone of the aerial top-dressing industry in this country, before they started building planes specifically for the job, like the Fletcher there.' He jerked his head towards the corrugated iron hangar across the grassy strip of runway and the small, rather ugly plane they had inspected first residing therein. 'Of course, we don't use Gertie here on the job any more, so Dave took the hopper off. Except for the paint job this is exactly how it looked when it was built in '45.'

Like the rest of the Tarrants, David was a multi-talent—musician, aircraft mechanic, mountain-climber. Naturally he was a flyer, too; even Beth could claim that distinction. Only Florence Tarrant preferred to keep her feet on solid ground, because, she confided to Fran with a twinkle, she suffered badly from motion sickness. She seemed to understand, though, what drove the rest of the family to seek adventure wherever they could find it. 'As long as they're happy' was her serene philosophy. Without it Fran didn't think she could have survived marriage to a man who, having retired early to let his sons run his business, had taken up stunt flying and helicopter search-and-rescue work to 'keep him on his toes'.

Fran couldn't help but wonder if there was a price for that outer serenity. How did she endure the waiting?

As Jason guided Fran on a complete circuit of the little yellow and black striped biplane on the pocket-airfield, she couldn't help thinking that she was rather involved in a waiting game herself...thanks to the man sauntering along behind them, hands thrust into the pockets of his faded jeans, wire-rimmed aviator sunglasses masking his expression. Why hadn't he followed through on that promise, that threat, to become her lover? Since Sunday lunch he had surrounded them with his family, and on the rare occasions that he and Fran *were* alone all he seemed to want to do was *talk*...long, lazy, rambling conversations that were fascinating, but pointless.

They began with Ross doing most of the talking, obligingly filling in the blank years, the years of study and striving, of hardship and success, of the crises, big and small, that marked out the progression of his maturity. He even spoke, lightly and whimsically, of his search for love: 'the one area where I have a very consistent failure rate, perhaps because I was looking in all the wrong places', although, he admitted with a crocodile grin, that failure had its compensations.

'I'll bet it has,' Fran had said darkly.

'Now, Fran, you've looked, too, and you should be grateful that I'm not a virgin, after your last experience with one...'

She had blushed at his teasing. His disarming, sometimes embarrassing, but always fascinating frankness had seduced Fran into a similar honesty. She had told him about her abortive affair with the medical student, but not that it had been her first *and* last experience. However, the wryness with which she had described her disillusionment told him far more than she knew. It had made him certain that, however many—or few—men she had been to bed with, none of them had been lovers in the true sense of the word. She had been no closer to love than he, and the passion in her nature was still largely untapped. Fran would need her emotions engaged, as well as her senses, before she gave herself fully to any man.

Fran quite enjoyed the mutual exploration of character, except when Ross spoke with chilling passion of his exploits in competition sky-diving and his growing interest in hang-gliding and micro-lite planes. But each night she went to bed restless and unsatisfied, and amused by her own perversity. Here was a man showing an interest in her mind and all she wanted him to do was hustle her into bed!

'Ready to go up?'

'What? Oh, sure,' Francesca shook free of her indecisive thoughts. 'Which one are we going up in?' She looked back at the Fletcher and the small Cessna beside it.

'Why, this one, of course!' Jason chuckled as he patted the wooden propellor of the biplane.

Francesca blanched. 'You mean, it still *flies*?' Tessa and David, who had been standing to one side discussing invoices—Tessa did the books for this, and other small companies—grinned. Were they all in on the joke?

'Of course it does!' Jason looked mildly offended. 'This is a classic, you know. Dave will keep her flying as long as he can find parts to fit...or can jury-rig them. The RAF used to use these little babies as trainers, you know, because they're so sensitive. Put your hand out into the slipstream and you can make the thing yaw...'

'Really?' Fran didn't know what a yaw was, but it sounded dangerous.

'Waggle to you, darling,' Ross said with an aggravatingly kind smile of condescension. Fran glared at him. She could hardly back down now, with the other three watching expectantly. Turning coward now could cost her a tiny measure of their respect and, she realised, that mattered...

Reluctantly she allowed the two men to help her into the front cockpit.

Immediately she panicked. 'What are all these controls for? I don't have to *do* anything, do I?'

'Not if you don't want to, Fran,' said Jason with a straight face that didn't hide his amusement. 'I don't think you're ready to go solo yet. Ross will do the flying from behind you.'

'*Ross* will?' She squirmed round in the cramped seat to look at the rear cockpit. Sure enough, there was Ross, wearing an old-fashioned leather flying helmet and looking for all the world like a vintage fighter ace. Her stomach plunged. 'I thought *you* were taking me up!' she wailed to Jason.

'Here, put these on. It can get cold up there, even on a nice day like this.' Jason thrust a warm hand-knitted hat and scarf into her shaky fingers. 'Now sit straight and I'll do your harness up for you. Don't fuss, Fran. Truth to tell, Ross is a better flyer than Dave or I put together, it just wasn't what he wanted to do for a living...'

Francesca closed her eyes for the take-off. The plane was made of wood and wire and what felt like paper...it couldn't possibly fly! When she dared open her eyes her stomach rolled furiously at the angle of their ascent. Remembering Jason's comment about the plane's sensitivity, she sat rigidly still, white-knuckled hands clenched around the safety harness, trying to regulate the great gulps of cold air which kept slipstreaming into her

mouth. Gradually, as the engine continued to drone reassuringly, and the wings stayed on, and her stomach
adjusted to the sudden jolts of up and down draughts,
she began to relax and look about her. After ten minutes
she stopped thinking about how far down the ground
was and started thinking about how artificial it looked,
toy farms and clockwork animals on green-quilted
squares. After another ten minutes she was actually enjoying herself and ready to admit that Ross might have
done the right thing in tricking her into going up in this
jaunty little plane.

She was quite sorry when she saw the corrugated arch
of the hangar with 'Tarrant' painted on it in large red
letters appear below them. She turned gingerly in her
seat and looked back. The ace in the pilot's seat gave
her a cocky thumbs-up signal which she returned with
a laugh that was snatched away by the wind. Ross made
some more gestures with his hand, and thinking that he
meant to tell her they were going to land she smiled and
nodded and turned to brace herself, excitement and fear
gripping her with equal strength.

But instead of tilting down, the nose of the plane tilted
up so that Francesca found herself staring straight into
the muzzle of a blue sky. There was only one reason she
could think of as to why they were going up rather than
down, but Fran didn't believe that even Ross would do
that to her.

She was wrong.

She screamed for the entire duration of the stunt.
When they were upside down she closed her eyes and
screamed. She screamed when the loop passed into a
series of barrel rolls and the horizon spun dizzily on its
axis. She screamed in fear and outrage and sheer, helpless
fury. If she hadn't been too utterly terrified to move
anything but her vocal chords, she would have climbed

over into the rear cockpit and strangled the reckless idiot there before he could deny her the pleasure by killing them both.

The landing was an anticlimax. Francesca climbed out of the tiny torture chamber and stood still for a moment until she was sure that all her parts were in working order. Then she turned to confront the brazen, laughing confidence of the man who had almost caused her heart failure.

'Did you enjoy the roller-coaster ride? Sorry if you got a fright, but I knew that once——'

Her working parts worked perfectly. Her slap nearly took his head off. Throat still raw from screaming, Fran didn't bother to say a single word, she let her back say it for her. She stormed over to Ross's pick-up, which was parked on the roadside next to the hangar, slammed into the driver's seat and took off in a whirlwind of dust along the unsealed road, ignoring the shouts behind her. Let Ross hitch a ride back with his brother. It would serve him right if she wiped this old rust-bucket out doing a few fancy driving 'stunts'!

It wasn't until she was half-way back to the cabin that reaction overtook her and she began to shake, and to have difficulty keeping the car on the road. She almost went straight past the Tarrant driveway, but at the last minute turned in, not really knowing why. Ross's home should be the last place she should run to, but when she stumbled into the warm kitchen to find Florence Tarrant sitting down to a quiet cup of tea she knew why she had come. She might be Ross's mother, but she would understand...

'I won't bother apologising for my son's behaviour, Fran,' the older woman said, plying Fran with a soothing brand of tea and sympathy after listening to her unexpected visitor's disjointed tale of woe. 'He's quite capable of doing that for himself. A pity he's got too big to put over my knee.'

'I took care of that,' Fran confessed, the slight sting in her hand recalling the slap. It probably hurt her more than it did him. 'He *knew* I'd never been up in a small plane before. He *knew* that I was nervous, that I thought Jason was going to take me up in something enclosed and modern and . . . and . . . then he leads me like a lamb to slaughter and does those *awful* things . . .' She shivered at the memory of the rushing wind, the wild, cartwheeling world.

'I know it's no consolation, dear, but Ross is so used to stunting that he probably doesn't think of it as frightening or dangerous. Perhaps he thought you would find it thrilling, perhaps he was just showing off, trying to impress you with his skill.'

'He doesn't *have* to impress me! cried Fran furiously, not realising what she was revealing to his interested mother. Just having him kiss and touch her was breathtaking thrill enough . . . how much *more* impressive could he be? 'What would you have done, if he had done that to you?'

Florence Tarrant sipped her tea thoughtfully. 'I would have been sick all over him,' she said drily.

Suddenly they were laughing, Fran's high-pitched giggles semi-hysterical with relief. This mixture of sympathy and humour was just what she had needed to restore her perspective. 'I suppose it was rather funny,' she chuckled grudgingly. 'Me, screaming like a banshee, hanging from my shoulder-straps. If I'd seen it in a movie I would have thought it great fun. And you should have seen his face when I took off in his car, leaving him choking in a cloud of dust in the middle of the road. Now *that* was like a movie, *Keystone Cops* variety. I half expected him to chase after me.' That set them off again, until Fran remembered that he might well be chasing after her. She felt too confused and angry to face him quite yet. She pushed her empty cup away and jumped nervously to her feet.

'You won't tell him I laughed?' she said tentatively.

'I think he deserves a good long bit of grovelling first, wouldn't you say?' Florence Tarrant asked, her eyes still filled with serene merriment at her son's expense.

'More than a little,' growled Francesca darkly. 'And if he thinks he can just walk back into that cabin and jolly me into forgetting it, he's got another think coming!'

'I'll make up his bed here,' his mother offered, perfectly understanding, but privately doubting that the bed would be used. 'I take it that you won't stay on for dinner...Ross thought you might.'

Another indication that he didn't want to be alone with her. Fran stiffened at the sharp disappointment that knifed in her breast. 'No, thank you.' The thought of food at this particular time made her feel ill anyway, and the thought of facing Ross in her present state, without knowing what kind of mood he would be in, was enough to make her stutter, 'But...do you think...could you keep him——'

'He invited himself for dinner, he can stay for dinner,' Mrs Tarrant said firmly. 'I'll tell him that you both need time to cool off. And if you take his car and I make sure that he can't get any transport from here, well...that should slow him down somewhat.' She gave Fran a gentle, warning smile. 'But, short of chaining him up, we can't stop him if he's determined. And Ross on a mission is a very determined man...'

'No more determined than *I* can be.' The stubborn line to the young woman's chin reminded Florence so sharply of her eldest son that she had to hide another smile as she bid her farewell. The two of them made an interesting combination, and although Ross had always jealously guarded his bachelorhood a mother could always hope...

The clouds building up in thick, dark columns in the western sky brought an early dusk which suited Francesca's mood. She vented her initial wrath by packing up every stray possession of Ross's that she could find and dumping the lot out on the back porch. She had been right to have her doubts. It was lunacy to imagine that she and Ross could put aside their differences long enough to have any kind of amicable relationship. And to think that she had been on the verge of giving in to lust...no, actually *mourning* the fact that *he* seemed to be having second thoughts.

Funny side or not, what he had done this afternoon was a gross violation of her trust, and she refused to become the lover of a man who threatened to give her a coronary every time she ventured outside with him. Lurking beneath the pleasant, teasing character of the past few days was a daredevil monster champing at the bit to fling himself into another terrifying endeavour. Talk about Jekyll and Hyde...Ross was positively schizophrenic! On the one hand he was a mature, responsible doctor with an admirable reputation, on the other an incurable thrill-seeker. While Fran could imagine herself satisfying the one, she could never, in a million years of trying, satisfy the other. Cooped up here in convalescence, Ross had probably decided that he could 'make do' with Fran for feminine company, but out in the real world no doubt he required vibrant, exciting women, sophisticated and outgoing, the kind of women who make good race-track groupies or knife-thrower's assistants, Fran thought sourly. He was probably sitting at his parents' table right now, eating and drinking and laughing, relieved that he had escaped the toils of staid and boring Francesca Lewis. Perhaps it had been only pity in the first place, and he had merely pretended to want her because she had been so embarrassingly inept at hiding her inexplicable desire for this oh-so-desirable man! Fran cringed at the thought. She needed a drink—a large one. She was annoyed to find her hands shaking as she tried to extract the ice-cubes from the tray, dropping them all over the bench in the process. Perhaps that flight had been a deliberate attempt on Ross's part to frighten her off. Yes, that would appeal to his twisted mind! And now he was congratulating himself at having——

She gave a little scream as the sliding door to the deck shivered violently open. Ross stood there, scowling furiously at her, his hair damp and matted, jaw tense, sloppy sweatshirt showing dark circles under his arms.

'What in hell did you run away for?'

Fran controlled her well stoked fury with difficulty. How dared he make *her* sound like the guilty party? She drew herself up. 'Your stuff is on the back porch.'

'Typical, just typical,' Ross sneered, stepping into the room, big and menacing, breathing hard. 'Ignore a problem and it doesn't exist, huh, Fran? Well, Princess, *I'm* not going to ignore it. We're going to have this out if I have to——'

He was cut short by an ice-cube. It bounced off the hard angle of his chin, slithered down his chest and clattered on to the wooden floor. There was utter silence as the blue eyes narrowed dangerously. Fran swallowed nervously. She shouldn't have done that, but at least it had shut him up.

'That's the second time you've hit me today, lady!' Ross's voice was a purring threat. 'And that's one time too many.' He took another step forward.

'You stay where you are!' Fran squeaked, scrabbling among the ice-cubes, half-excited, half-terrified at her temerity, and still furious with him. She brandished a fistful of hard, icy missiles as she backed away. 'Ross, I'm warning you, I want you to take your things and get out——'

'Warning, Frankie?' he asked softly, still coming. 'Or bluffing . . . ?'

He didn't think she would do it! He thought she'd back down like a frightened rabbit just because he was bigger than she was. He thought he knew her well enough to predict her every move. He had a surprise coming!

Unfortunately the surprise didn't stop him. Fielding the raining chunks of ice, Ross caught her by the back door, ignoring her screams as he manhandled her out of the kitchen, forcing her to dump her last handful of ice-cubes on the floor, where they crunched underfoot as she wriggled helplessly in his purposeful arms.

'Let me go, you big bully!' Fran shrieked, kicking out with her dangling legs. Staggering slightly, Ross's foot came down on a stray ice-cube and skated out from under him. They both landed on the icy floor with a bone-shattering thump. Luckily Fran was on top, but when she caught her breath and tried to move she felt Ross's chest rise against her back in a thick groan.

'Ross? Are you all right?' Another groan. 'Are you hurt?' Carefully she eased herself sideways in his loosening arms and turned to face him, her hands automatically going over him, checking for injuries, anger forgotten in her anxiety. When she felt the rapid thud of his heart her fingers paused over the reassuring vibration.

'Don't stop . . .'

Her hands stiffened against his chest, but were caught and held by his. 'Ross Tarrant——' she began accusingly, but her words dried up when she tangled with his gaze: soft, blue, gentle...

'Compassion, Princess, it gets you every time, doesn't it? You'd care for the devil himself if he were hurt.'

'I think that's what I'm doing now,' she said drily, in an attempt to resist that melting tenderness.

'Not a devil, Frankie, just a man... and an exhausted one at that.' He sensed her fading anger and was careful not to smile. 'Mum'll never forgive me for leaving dinner on the table, but it suddenly occurred to me that you might take it into that muddled head of yours to run away, so I took off across the back fields. Ran all the way... in pretty good time, too!'

'You *ran*? In the *dark*? But it's *miles*!' Fran was both flattered and appalled. 'You could have fallen and broken your neck and lain there all night! My God, you're a menace to yourself as well as to other people.'

'You and Mum didn't leave me much choice,' he said apologetically. 'She even got Dad to hide the keys to the ride-on mower.'

Fran refused to laugh, and his loosely clasped hands at the back of her waist tightened as she stirred fretfully against his big body.

'Ah, Princess, don't look at me like that,' he sighed. 'I've already been told by Jason and Tessa and David how grossly cruel and thoughtless it was to spring those stunts on you. Tessa said I deserved the right cross. And my mother has subjected me to a harrowing hour of silent reproach. I didn't mean to frighten you, Fran. I just got carried away. You were so obviously enjoying the flight, I just wanted to share the fantastic feeling of freedom I get rolling around the sky——'

'Yes, *you* get. *You*,' Fran said tautly, thankful that she hadn't had that drink after all. He wasn't going to find her so forgiving this time. 'Not me! You weren't trying to share, you were trying to force that feeling on me, regardless of what I wanted. I'm not like you and I don't want to be. If what I am isn't good enough for you, well, that's too bad. I'm not changing my entire personality just to accommodate your whims.' Yes, that sounded good, reasonable but firm, with just the right element of subtle accusation. Perhaps too subtle. 'Your *temporary* whims.'

He could hardly miss that thickly significant look and tone. The sober expression with which he had greeted her unarguable statement of independence sharpened. 'Are you implying what I *think* you're implying?' he asked slowly.

Fran lifted her eyebrows haughtily. 'I don't know. What do you think I'm implying?' The haughtiness backfired, for it made him grin.

'That my wanting to make love to you was just a fleeting whim. My God, woman, are you insane? Whatever gave you that stupid idea?'

A hot, sweet pang pierced Fran's body at his incredulous growl. 'You're the one who turned cool all of a sudden,' she retaliated defensively.

'Cool? Is that what you thought?' He gave a laughing groan. 'Frankie, if my temperature was any higher I'd spontaneously combust! I was *trying* to leave the next move up to you. It was obvious that you had doubts, and I thought you needed a little time to work them through.' He chuckled ruefully at the wild blush that flooded over her stunned face. 'Shame on you, my liberated young businesswoman! Were you only waiting for me to sweep you off your feet? I didn't think there was any mad rush. After all, we do live in the same city...'

Fran felt a squeezing pain in her chest, followed by a panicky flutter. What did he mean by that? She had been torturing herself with erotic imaginings for days, gearing herself up to a brief holdiay fling and hoping that it would rid her of this dangerous, unreasoning obsession she had developed for him. Wasn't that what he had wanted? What they both had wanted? There had been no mention of a future. The idea of an open-ended affair was slightly terrifying. Could she handle it? Did she dare risk the physical and emotional disruption he would inevitably create in her life? She paused on the brink of a great discovery, but his next words buried it again under an avalanche of riotous sensation.

'You know...what I do up there in the air,' he murmured in a voice that had the texture of cut velvet, 'the "high" it gives me, is the next best thing to sex. Perhaps this afternoon was a subconscious attempt to sublimate my *real* need...to do this...' He slowly eased over until he was braced above Fran's supine body, his hips lowering to grind softly against her thighs until they parted to allow him to lie between, the rough denim weave of his jeans catching against the soft wool-blend of her slacks. '...and I needed you up there, with me, to share the exhilaration, the agony and the ecstasy of subliminal sex. God, Frankie, how much longer are you going to make us wait? Tell me, tell me you want me to touch you, and taste you, and feed your appetite with mine...'

With a cry of need that echoed his own, Fran arched against him. His musky male scent was strong in her nostrils, his tongue knowledgeable and exquisitely familiar in her mouth. In a wondrously compelling feat of strength he stood up, supporting their combined weights without taking his mouth off hers. Then she felt his torso slide and dip against her breasts, and clutched at his baggy sweater as she felt herself being swept off her feet. It seemed appropriate.

'No, Ross, put me down...I'm too heavy for you. Your arm...' her mouth escaped his to plead, even as she revelled in the possessive gesture.

He looked down at her, all arrogant male pride for an instant, until she saw the softness in the big, blue-grey eyes. Then he chuckled and whirled her around a couple of times with a speed that made her gasp and shut her eyes, it was so reminiscent of her recent flight. When she opened them they were in the darkened bedroom.

'I love the way you care,' he said with a voice full of warmth and desire as he nuzzled the opening of her blouse.' All stiff and starchy and bossy on the outside, but inside soft and buttery, slightly salty and slightly sweet...' He licked her skin and Fran's soft and buttery insides began to sizzle. 'But you're right, after all the alarms and excursions of today I do feel rather weak. Shall we lie down together and tend each other's wounds, heal each other...?' He lowered her to the firm resilience of the bed, following her down, plucking at the clothes that suddenly seemed rough and hurtful against her skin, barriers to his sexual healing. Her own blind touch found his skin under the sweatshirt, damp and hot to the touch, a series of smooth undulations of bone and muscle.

'Do I feel cool to you now, Princess?' he growled huskily when her clothes lay discarded on the floor and his shadowy bulk rose over her, clad only in narrow, dark briefs. 'Is that why you shiver?' his voice teased her while his hand explored what he uncovered with erotic slowness. 'Shall I warm you, Princess...here...and here?' His delicate touch sent another sighing quiver through her body. 'Ah, Frankie, at last... after all these years...'

Just as she was sinking beyond rational thought, Ross pulled back and twisted his body to reach up to the light switch on the wall above them.

'No——' Fran caught him just in time, feeling a sudden return of shyness, an echo of the past. She wanted to be perfect for him, and the only way that she could be that was if he couldn't see her as she really was. True, she wasn't plump any more, but the image of herself still remained...

'No?' He let her guide his hand away, but grasped instead the curtains beside the bed and dragged them back so that the pale light of a full moon spilled over the tumbled bed. Its light was enchantingly revealing, yet Fran didn't feel exposed. Moonlight was romantic, kind, silvering away imagined imperfections.

'Ah, Princess, how could you try to deny me the pleasure of watching myself make love to you?' he murmured with throaty satisfaction, his shadowed eyes running over the moon-bleached smoothness of her body, the breasts that fascinated him with their lush femininity, the pearly sheen of her thighs where they curved invitingly inwards.

Slowly he reached out to cup her breast with an almost reverent desire. He knelt beside her, his other hand joining worship of her breasts, the muscles in his belly and thighs tensing as he watched them respond to his flattery, swelling in his hands, the taut nipples beckoning his mouth. As his head dipped in homage, Francesca saw the explicit outline of his need, held straining captive by the thin strip of silk across his loins. She gasped, digging her fingers into the broad, bowed shoulders in a sharp agony of wanting. When she felt his mouth, exquisitely gentle, tasting, enveloping her in warm wetness, violent sensation exploded in the pit of her belly, radiating out through her body in rippling waves of shock.

As he made love to her breasts with his skilful mouth, he nudged her flat on the bed, his hands straying down to twine her legs against him until she could no longer bear the separation and tugged at the silk on his hips with trembling fingers, silently begging him to help her. With an easy flex of muscle he bent and stripped off his briefs, then angled himself against her on the narrow bed to provide them with fleeting relief from the growing pressure in both their bodies.

'Yes, Francesca...God, yes!' he cried gratingly as she moved her thighs restlessly against his velvety hardness, teasing his pulsating desire, finding him with her hands and marvelling at his hot virility. The moonlight played across their shifting bodies, a cool counterpoint to the heat they were generating, and Fran was naïvely astonished at how exciting it was to see as well as to feel what Ross was doing to her, and she to him. Her experience of sex had been of a rushed sense of urgency too soon satisfied...this slow, languid, sensuously thorough journey of exploration was a revelation. Her wide-eyed delight provoked her lover to even greater pleasures and, when at last his strong, gentle fingers lingered, breath-soft on the delicate flesh between her quivering thighs, Fran was stormed by a violent, racking shudder that almost spilled him from his position of dominance. His hand wrapped around her hips, holding her still.

'No...wait, Francesca...' He sucked in his breath. '...slow down...'

'I...can't...' She twisted helplessly, unable to control her body's demand as he groaned against her.

'I don't think I can either...' He thrust her legs apart with a possessive strength that sent a stab of pain to the core of her pleasure. Then, just as he moved between her legs his body clenched. 'Oh, damn...I...I'm not prepared... You are on the pill, aren't you?'

It was a question that had no meaning and the manner of his asking made the answer a mere formality, but Francesca stiffened, her hands balling against his back. The pill? Contraception? Until that instant what they were doing together had had no relevance to anything else, much less to the act of procreation. Sex? Babies? Suddenly the true meaning of what they were risking hit her like a hurricane...

'No!' Babies should be born out of mutual love, not selfish passion. Fran would never, never bring a child into the world unwanted by either parent, as her mother had done. A love child... what bitter irony in the name.

'No?' Ross's voice was hoarse, uncomprehending, his body freezing rigid when his brain interpreted her reply. *'No?'*

'No.' She closed her eyes against the tears, and the terrible realisation, unable to prevent the words tumbling out, 'I'm not used to this sort of thing, you see. I'm not *experienced...*'

'Don't, Frankie——' He rolled off her with a groan and pulled her hard against the length of him, cupping her chin in his hand and forcing her to look at him. 'Don't you think I know that? That's why it's important that this be good for you, why I wanted you to be *sure.*' He gave a short, stunned laugh, blue eyes expressing his bewilderment. 'I can't believe this...I was so busy trying to blind you with the rightness of our being lovers that I didn't even think of the elementary precautions. If this ridiculous situation is anyone's fault it's mine... contraception is part of my *business*, for God's sake!'

'Perhaps it was a Freudian slip, perhaps you didn't really want——'

'Baby, you have to be kidding!' He cut off her attempt to ease away from him with a very definite movement of his still-aroused body against hers and closed his eyes with a slight shudder. 'I'm very, very tempted to ask if this is a safe time for you——' his voice was thick and slow, like syrup '—but we're both too intelligent to deny the element of risk.' He opened his eyes and looked at her and smiled, a slow, sultry smile of resignation. 'Ah, well, Princess, if the path of pleasure is barred to us, I guess we'll have to dally in the by-ways...'

'No, please...can you...just hold me?' Fran put a frantic hand against the deep chest. She knew to suggest that he leave would provoke a confrontation that she couldn't endure, and to have him make half-love to her would be even worse. She held her breath when he studied her flushed face long and hard, her fearful grey eyes and trembling mouth. He protested, but tenderly, with a gentleness that made her ache, and at last acquiesced and held her until the awful tension drained away. They talked of inconsequential things, Francesca desperately willing him to sleep, and when at last the big naked body slackened in sleep she lay there in an agony of guilt for what she was going to do. He had held her, rocked away the pain, acted with supreme consideration in putting her needs above his...all the time believing that tomorrow, tomorrow she would fulfil *his* needs. She was cheating him, and he would never forgive her. But it was for the best...it had to be for the best!

CHAPTER NINE

FRAN was in the bath when the doorbell rang. She groaned. Her nightly soak was the one leisurely luxury she afforded herself in her current hectic, dawn-to-dusk schedule. It was also a necessity, for she came home each night weary, sweaty, grimy and often delicately perfumed with manure. If she didn't love it so much she would bemoan the success of The Garden Company, so completely did it devour her life. But the hard work was worth it. In three short, yet also very long, months she and Christina had built up a booming business, confounding not only their critics but also their own cautious expectations.

Fran towelled herself quickly, grimacing as she caught sight of the bedroom clock. Eight-thirty. The few of her friends who hadn't been driven off by her inhospitable hours knew better than to make social calls after dark. Fran was often in bed at this time, trying to wrest sleep away from regretful, disturbing dreams.

The soft pink and grey tracksuit clung uncomfortably to her still-damp skin, but Fran was too tired to care. She would get rid of whoever it was, heat a quick TV dinner and fall into bed.

She was yawning as she opened the front door of her apartment, leaving the safety chain attached. The yawn froze in her throat.

'Beth!'

Fran fumbled with the chain and threw the door wide, her eyes automatically going past the hesitantly smiling girl to the echoingly empty corridor beyond. Her stomach twisted. What had she expected? She had made it very clear to Ross that she didn't want to see him again, and he had as much pride as she did.

The painful thought must have shown in her face because Beth Tarrant's smile faded and she shifted her bag awkwardly from one shoulder to the other.

'Hello, Fran...I know I should have rung first but...well, Mum did give me your address and said you asked about me when you wrote. She said I should look you up...I was just on my way back to the hostel from the movies, and since I was passing——' The girl shrugged and tried another smile. 'Look, if I've come at a bad time, I can come back...' She half turned away.

'No!' Fran's urgent cry surprised them both. 'I mean, it's lovely to see you, Beth. I was just surprised, that's all.' In those last few golden days at Whaler's Bay she and Beth had become quite friendly, the teenager confiding her firm intention to start her nursing training in Auckland as soon as she was old enough. 'Come on through. Excuse the faint air of neglect,' she apologised, with the guilt of former fastidiousness for the comfortably furnished but untidy lounge. 'I've been so flat out I really only use this place for washing, eating and sleeping...in that order.'

'You live here alone?'

'I used to share with another nurse, but when she moved out to get married I didn't bother to find anyone else. I can afford the rent and I appreciate the peace and quiet.' Fran hoped that Beth didn't notice the slight ring of hollowness. Since the girl looked interested she showed her around. Beth seemed strangely subdued and diffident, quite unlike her usual bouncy self.

'When did you start your training?' Fran asked, as the tour finished up in the second bedroom and Beth showed the first glimmer of her former animation.

'Three weeks ago today. Of course it'll be ages before I'm allowed near real patients.' She sighed. Was she disillusioned already? Fran could have sworn that Beth had the enthusiasm, determination and resilience to make a good nurse. It was all she had ever wanted to be, she had told Fran, with that Tarrant confidence.

'Would you like some tea or coffee? I was just about to heat myself some dinner...'

'I'm a bit peckish myself,' Beth said with engaging wistfulness. 'I'm paying full board at the hostel, but the meal hours are fixed and if you miss out, you miss out. The biddy who runs it doesn't like us mucking about too much in her kitchen, so other than snacks I don't get a chance to cook the things I like.' Beth had her mother's flair in the kitchen and Fran, having tasted some of her offerings, could appreciate the mournful look.

''I was only going to heat up something frozen, but you can make us some of your fancy omelettes if you like.'

Fran showed her where everything was in the compact kitchen and then set the oval table, listening in amusement to Beth's rapid-fire chatter as she whirled from fridge to bench to stove, her long, dark plait flying around her slim shoulders.

'I would have called ages ago.' Beth raised her voice over the whisking of eggs. 'But I wasn't quite sure of my welcome. I know that you and Ross had some kind of fight...'

'Yes, we did...but you're always welcome to call in, Beth,' Fran managed to keep her voice even. 'A lot of my work involves beavering away on my own, so I appreciate a bit of company.' It was as close as she'd come to admitting she was a little lonely. Success was sweet, but it would be sweeter with someone to share it.

Christine, as a solo mother of two teenage children, had a very busy life outside the running of the seven-day-a-week Garden Centre, and the assistant who helped Fran with the contracting was also studying horticulture, so she didn't see much of them in her off-hours. Now that she had begun to adjust to the new rhythms of her life, Fran had the awful feeling that she was going to miss Ross even more...

Ross. To say that they had had a fight wasn't quite accurate. *She* had fought, Ross had reasoned, but Fran had been in no mood to listen to reason. She had been afraid, and as always when she was afraid she had closed up and listened only to the promptings of her fear. In all his sweet seduction Ross had never murmured a word of love. He had been honest. There had been no embarrassing slip of the tongue to encourage false hopes, he had spoken only of mutual needs and desires. Oh yes, Fran had those, but her close encounter with the white heat of her own passion had shaken her deeply. That she was capable of such unreserved feeling was frightening, and realising that she had fallen in love with him against the dictates of her own will was even more disturbing. The strength of her feelings made a mockery of her fond belief that she could handle a brief holiday affair with Ross. Or a long one, that would be even worse...storing up pain for herself day by day, week by week, until Ross got bored with her acquiescence and sought new challenges, new adventures, and returned her love with its legacy of bitter interest. He might demand no more of her than passion, but her own hunger for loving would demand that she give him everything, try and purchase his love with hers. In doing so she would lose a vital part of herself, her self-respect...turn into the kind of woman who pursued passion blindly, relentlessly hopeful, relentlessly disappointed. No, Fran wanted to be master of her own fate, not a mistress in someone else's...

So instead of awakening to a new day with a new lover in his arms, Ross had padded out into the lounge next morning, lazy and sensuous as a cat, to find Fran packing, her defences honed razor-sharp by the fear of what those penetrating blue eyes would see.

He had been justifiably incredulous at her announcement that she had decided that she had been neglecting her 'real life' for too long. At first he had been teasing, then coaxing, then stunningly sincere as he suggested that *he* help her solve her 'real life' problems. Instead of her worrying about probate being settled, why didn't *he* underwrite her loan? Hell, he would loan her the money himself, at a far better rate than the bank allowed her...and that would mean that instead of selling the cabin they could keep it on as a weekend hide-away.

Fran had exploded. So that was what he wanted...a hole-in-the-corner affair, a weekend lover who wouldn't intrude into the rest of his life! Well, he had intruded too far into hers already. It wasn't enough that he had summarily invaded her heart, now he was trying to muscle in on the only thing of her own that she truly and freely possessed...her dream. He was buying an affair, but not with love...with his *money*. Talking as if he had some right to a stake in her future.

She had said bitter things and he had responded with a withering contempt that seemed to see straight through her feverish rejection of any kind of involvement between them.

'My God, is this the way you usually function, Fran? Slitting the throat of a relationship before it can make any real demands on you?'

'What sort of demands were you thinking of making?' She had meant to make it sound sarcastic, but it came out horrifyingly like a plea.

'Oh, no, Fran.' He shook his head, voice soft and veined with cynicism. 'No free rides. You pays your money and you takes your choice. You'll never know if you don't take the plunge with me. Human relationships don't come with written guarantees.'

'I'm not asking for guarantees,' she denied furiously. 'Certainly not from a man like you. Sooner or later you're going to break your crazy neck in one of your stunts and leave those unfortunate enough to care about you high and dry.'

His eyes narrowed and she turned away, afraid that she had revealed too much. 'Would you have me different, Fran?'

If he had been different she probably wouldn't have fallen in love with him and she wouldn't be suffering now. 'Yes.'

He walked around her rigid back and confronted her with a weary resignation that battered more fiercely at her bruised heart than had his earlier angry contempt. 'What do you want me to do? Make you pretty promises that neither of us would believe? In between last night and this morning, Princess, you misplaced some of that fine courage of yours. Last night we discovered things about each other, elemental things...this morning you act as if that makes us enemies. Is being so close to another human being so terrifying, Fran? You're not running *to* anything as much as away from it. You've locked yourself into one set of options and it has blinded you to others. We all have to live with compromises, Fran, small and large...if we don't bend to life we break. The bottom line here is that *I'm* prepared to take a risk on us, to nurture growth, and you're not. What do you really want, Fran? Do you know? If you get what you think you want, will it be enough?'

'Yes.' Defiant to the last.

So he had let her walk out of his life, speeding her on her way with one last, poison-tipped barb that had pierced her armoured emotions.

'If you change your mind about what you want, look me up. But don't wait too long, Princess. Unlike you, I don't fight what I am—a human being with passions and physical appetites, and a human need for emotional as well as physical intimacy...'

'What's the matter, don't you like it?'

'What? Oh!' Fran blinked at the omelette on the table in front of her and picked up her fork to taste. 'It's delicious, Beth. Sorry, I was miles away.'

Brooding. She couldn't stop herself indulging in the torture of speculation. Where was Ross now? What was he doing? Had he found someone else already to stimulate his wretched human appetite? If he hadn't...

'So, how's life in general treating you?' she asked Beth, firmly crushing her mind's treachery.

'Oh, great, the course is really terrific.' Beth chattered on, but Fran was jolted out of her own jealous self-absorption by the realisation that the younger girl was straining for the right note of cheer, and she mentioned nothing of her personal life.

'Beth, everything is all right, isn't it?' she interrupted gently.

'Sure. Great!' Her cheerfulness wavered under the steady grey stare and suddenly her shoulders slumped. 'Does it show? Oh, Fran...I guess that's really why I came. I just don't know what to do...'

Oh no, thought Fran wryly, *not you, too.* 'Have you discovered that nursing isn't what you want to do, after all? It's nothing to be ashamed of, Beth, better now than——'

'It's not that,' Beth wailed. 'I love the nursing part. It's just that...that...Fran, it's so *awful* living in that *institution...*' It all came tumbling out. Beth had never been away from home and family before, and she was bitterly homesick. 'Don't tell me it'll pass, everyone tells me that and I know it's only a phase, but sometimes I really feel like chucking it all in!' she finished with dramatic misery.

Fran, to whom hostel living had been a pleasant change from the strict discipline and loneliness of home, nevertheless sympathised.

'Couldn't you have gone and lived with Ross?' The name, unspoken for months, stuck to her tongue lovingly and she had to force herself to continue. 'Instead of going to a hostel?''

'Ross lives about forty-three bus changes away from Tech,' Beth exaggerated glumly, 'and we have quite a few evening classes. He works all sorts of hours, too, so I probably wouldn't see any more of him than I do now. He's so busy...and when he does get time to himself I don't suppose he wants a kid sister hanging around to cramp his style.' She clapped a hand over her stricken mouth in horror. 'I'm sorry, Fran, I forgot——'

'I wish I could,' Fran said wryly, and smiled to show her there were no hard feelings. At times, Beth's impulsiveness got the better of her tact.

'Anyway, I made such a terrible song and dance about being able to cope, boasting about striking out on my own, I'm-not-a-baby-any-more and so on, because Mum wanted me to stay with Aunty Celia who is nice enough in small doses but is practically a certified loony on the subject of what 'nice girls' don't do—mainly, have any fun at *all*...that I just *can't* go bawling to Ross. It would be so humiliating, and brothers can be rottenly un-sympathetic, you know. Oh, Fran, what am I going to *do*?' A tearful plea, full of such trusting belief in her power to make things right was more than Fran could resist.

She sighed. 'I suppose you could stay here. The second bedroom is——'

'Oh, Fran, really? You life-saver! You darling!' Beth's heartfelt relief clutched at her before the words were out of her mouth. 'Mum'll be so chuffed! I think she was starting to read between the lines a bit...and she likes you and thinks you're really responsible...what a fan-tastic solution! You really are a darling to come up with it...though I must admit that when I saw that spare room I might have done a teensy weensy bit of subtle angling,' she grinned, her naturally sunny self re-adjusting to the new situation. 'Oh, Fran, you'll hardly even notice I'm here, I promise, and we'll have such *fun*...!'

The first wasn't at all true, but because of the second Fran found that the loss of her precious peace and quiet was much outweighed by the pleasures of Beth's company. Occasionally, with a look or a gesture or a remark, Beth would conjure up a stinging likeness to her eldest brother that struck Fran into speechless longing, but for the most part she added a dimension to Fran's life that had been missing. Beth was the sister she had never had, someone to take and give advice, someone to listen or moan to, to share small victories and defeats with, to go shopping with and giggle over the differences in taste. Because Fran refused to accept more from Beth than she had been paying in board at the hostel, the girl insisted on doing the lion's share of the housework, par-ticularly the cooking. Fran, in turn, helped Beth with her studies. Passing on the benefit of her knowledge and experience not only appeased her last lingering guilt about forsaking her nursing career, but also the more immediate guilt that she had her own less than altruistic motives for taking the girl under her wing; she wanted to see Ross again.

It wasn't working—trying to forget him. Oh, superficially her life was full and busy and increasingly successful, but there was a hollow ring to it, signalling an inner emptiness that only Ross could fill. She still loved him, after all these months of absence. In her heart, his image was still fresh and bright and vibrant. At times he seemed so close that she almost turned and said, 'Hey, look what I've done, aren't you proud of me?' And he would have been. Ross hadn't been trying to hold her back, or box her in, he had been trying to show her that the parameters of freedom were the ones she created for herself. She had boxed *herself* in by anticipating the worst and thus precipitating the prospect. There was much to be said for Ross's philosophy, which seemed to be a Tarrant trademark, of taking the optimistic approach to life, of believing the best of people rather than the worst.

But how to let Ross know that the decision to cut him unceremoniously out of her life, made in panic and haste, was being repented at leisure? What if he too had changed his mind? Or already moved on? Was that why Beth was being so aggravatingly and uncharacteristically tactful, carefully skirting the subject of Ross whenever his name slipped inadvertently into the conversation? Was that why Ross never visited his sister at the flat, or telephoned? Never passed on regards or even a greeting through the third party of his sister, or his mother? Fran knew that Beth spent some of her afternoons off in Ross's company because the girl was usually unnervingly honest about her doings. On the evenings that she clammed up about her activities Fran knew, with the jealous instinct of one who loved, that she had been with Ross. Knowing that he was out there, existing parallel to yet not touching her life, filled her with restless frustration. The solution, she knew, was in her own hands. She would have to make the first move. Perhaps, she told herself hopefully, this was another example of his determination that she abide by her own choices rather than his...

Her tension inevitably communicated itself to Beth, who became even more tiresomely tactful, until Fran told her tartly one morning to stop behaving as if her brother didn't exist.

'I was just following your lead,' Beth protested righteously, giving Fran's frustrated face an up-and-under look that was suspiciously innocent. 'I thought you weren't interested.'

'Well, you thought wrong,' Fran said pettishly. 'Your mother never mentions him either, when she writes. Is this conspiracy of silence carried out on Ross, too?'

Beth's blue eyes skittered away. 'N-o-o-o. Mum's told him all about The Garden Company and how well it's going, of course, but she said that we weren't to interfere...that you two had to work it out between yourselves...'

'It?' Fran's eyebrows rose sarcastically. Did Florence *want* Fran to have an affair with her son? She was always warm and friendly when she rang to check on her daughter...Fran noticed Beth's uncomfortable blush and regretted her sarcasm. It wasn't Beth's fault she was frustrated. 'We can hardly work it out when we never see each other...' She would just have to force herself into action, and the hell with pride. Love conquers all, she reminded herself sternly, and pretended to ignore Beth's furtive excitement.

That evening she was out in her walled courtyard, up to her elbows in potting mix when the doorbell rang. Expecting Beth, getting ready for a night on the town with one of her new-found city friends, to answer it with her usual eagerness, Fran brushed back a sweaty curl with one gloved hand, leaving a streak of dirt on her temple to match the one on her chin, and continued to re-pot. The bell rang twice more and Fran was half-way across the lounge, grumbling testily to herself when Beth popped out of her bedroom, clad in a towel.

'Fran, would you mind——? *Fran!* You can't answer the door like that...what happened to that nice dress you were wearing?'

'I didn't want to get it dirty,' Fran said mildly, looking down at the now extremely grubby stonewashed denims that Beth had persuaded her to buy, insisting that they should be half a size too small 'for effect', and the equally grubby, loose, once-white T-shirt that she had pulled on over her unfettered breasts. 'What's the matter,' she teased 'is it someone special? A man?'

'No, yes...' Beth hissed, looking as if she was about to start ringing her hands in despair as the doorbell sounded again. 'Fran, you don't understand...'

'I promise I won't frighten him off,' Fran said in amusement. Beth was usually terrifyingly blasé about her boyfriends. 'We have to let him in and you certainly can't do it like that. Stop fussing, Beth,' she scolded as the girl let out another anguished protest. 'If he looks down his nose at me I'll excuse myself and change, and if he turns out to be a nice guy he can come out and watch me pot my plants. Now go and finish dressing...I thought you were always ready *early* for dates.'

'Fran!' Beth's cry was despairing. 'At *least* take off the gardening gloves!'

'If he's as prissy as you seem to think I don't think he's going to want to shake hands anyway,' Fran called back with playful perversity. Beth was very fond of giving people 'snob tests', especially in up-market dress shops where she would suddenly lapse into excruciating country-bumpkinisms. Many a time Fran had been torn between laughter and embarrassment as she dragged her companion away. Perhaps tonight she could get her own back. Pinning a vacant smile to her lips, she threw the door wide.

It was Ross.

Wasn't it? She blinked. His thick hair was trimmed to glossy neatness and he was wearing a *suit*. It was dark, teamed with an immaculate silver-grey silk shirt and maroon tie, his raw masculinity refined into elegant, expensive lines that Fran had a savagely jealous urge to smudge, to turn him back into the Ross she knew.

'Ross...what are you doing here?' To her horror it came out almost like an accusation, when he had sacrificed his pride to come and see her...

'More to the point, what are *you* doing here?' he shocked her by replying. Suddenly she noticed the fine-grained skin pulled taut around the mouth and nose and eyes. He was as shocked as she was by this confrontation. But that would mean... 'I was under the impression that Beth was living at a student nurses' hostel. I appear to have been wrong,' he said, his voice coming out dry and lifeless as he looked beyond her into the flat, and the untidy signs of Beth's occupation.

Fran closed her eyes briefly as she assimilated his ignorance. Neither Beth nor his mother had told him. For weeks she had been plagued by the assumption that he had known but not wanted to make use of the knowledge. 'I...she moved out of the hostel weeks ago. Didn't she tell you?' She wavered unnecessarily. The sky-blue eyes came back to hers and locked on them relent-lessly. Her mouth dried as she watched them change from shock, to suspicion, to wariness, to an unreadable blankness.

'No, she didn't.'

Unnerved by the clipped reply, and the stillness of the big body, Fran found herself babbling out all Beth's troubles, stressing that Beth had come to *her*, not the other way around.

His mask of inexpression flickered at that, and for the first time he looked beyond her pale face. He looked at her hair, crimped by the spring humidity, the dirty streaks on her skin and revealing-concealing casual garb. She felt like a street urchin being looked over by a plutocrat, and unconsciously drew herself up to compensate with a haughty stare. A gleam fleetingly silvered the blue eyes and she stiffened. Did he find her funny? OK, so she was scruffy, but she had seen him look worse. She wasn't going to let him embarrass her, she wasn't ashamed of her body. He obviously noticed, from the way his eyes had lingered on the swell of her hips, that she wasn't as slim as she had been a few months ago, but her roundness wasn't fat. It was smooth, sleekly conditioned muscle. She was more supple and fitter than she had ever been in her life, thanks to the hard manual labour she was putting in.

'No need to get so uptight, Fran,' he drawled, as ner-vousness drove her on to restate Beth's case. 'I get the message. I'm not to take this as an oblique attempt on your part to fling yourself back into my arms.'

Since that was exactly what it had been, at least in part, Fran found herself flushing faintly. Was that relief she detected? She jutted her chin defensively.

'No wonder Beth never wanted me to run her back to the hostel, and only rang from Tech. I wonder who the secrecy was designed to protect? You or me?' He raised an eyebrow and his mouth curved slightly as he watched her wipe her palms nervously against her denim-clad thighs. Suddenly Fran caught a breathtaking glimpse of the man she knew, and an avalanche of feeling rushed into her hollow heart.

'Don't feel you need to apologise for having taken my sister under your wing, Francesca.' In the midst of that bland softness the drawn-out syllables of her name were an intimate caress that made her heart skip. 'I know that in spite of her brashness and the aura of confidence Beth carries around with her she's still vulnerable, and you're a sucker for vulnerability, aren't you? I have some very fond remembrances of your compassionate breast myself...' And he stared deliberately at the place where her heart thumped passionately beneath the thin white cotton. Oh, God, that look! Inexorably Fran felt the light, delicious tingling that pressaged the tender tautening of her breasts. Quickly she spun around, missing the leaping flare of satisfaction that brought a grimly predatory smile to Ross's lips. So... She was proud, and stubborn and still bristling with defences, but her body and those big, lonely eyes betrayed her. She ached for him as much as he ached for her. His patience had paid off. But, in view of the unexpected circumstances, he would have to take a different, more direct approach from the one he had planned.

'Come in—I'll just see if Beth is ready——' Fran said nervously, leading him into the lounge and turning towards the bedroom.

'Still running scared, Fran?' His soft taunt stopped her. 'Surely you don't intend to disappoint Beth after she's obviously gone to so much trouble to bring us together again?' When Fran still didn't turn around, he added, 'And it's a little late for a cover-up. If you're embarrassed by your body you only have yourself to blame. Women with breasts as sensitive as yours shouldn't go braless if they don't want their body language read...'

Fran turned proudly, gloved hands clenched at her sides to prevent them crossing defensively over her tingling breasts. 'I never denied that I found you attractive,' she said in a stifled voice.

'Only that it wasn't enough. I didn't agree at the time, but I do now. Not nearly enough.' His eyes glinted at her bewildered reaction to his cryptic remarks. 'You look quite beautiful, Frankie.'

She was taken aback by the sincerity of the quiet compliment. 'I... Don't be ridiculous, I'm a mess...'

He smiled, and a tongue of flame licked out of the blue eyes to singe her body beneath its flimsy covering. 'A beautiful mess... how I always imagined you'd look when you made peace with yourself... earthy, real, the kind of woman a man wants to enfold and be enfolded by...'

A slumberous warmth flushed across Fran's skin. Earthy, that's how she felt, especially when he looked at her like that, and her feelings for him were very strong and real. *Thank you, Beth*, she thought silently. The girl had enabled them to meet without sacrifice of pride on either side. 'I'm afraid I'm earthy in the very literal sense,' she said huskily, holding on to his gaze with difficulty. She *had* made peace with herself, and he was part of the treaty. She lifted her grimy-gloved hands apologetically. 'While you look very... elegant.'

She didn't understand why he laughed softly, until he explained. 'You make it sound like an accusation... after all the times you tried to make me put some clothes on when we lived together.' Fran's flush heated even more at the images his turn of phrase presented and his voice deepened, catching her off guard. 'It's just a skin, and underneath it I'm just the same man...a little more lean and hungry maybe, but the same man. I missed you, Princess. Did you miss me?'

He didn't wait for an answer. His hand reached out to cup the heavy fullness of one breast and exert the pressure which guided her body forward against his as his mouth covered hers, searching and finding her melting response.

As he kissed her his hand massaged her breast in lazy circles until she moaned quietly, and he lifted his mouth to murmur, 'Touch me... You want to, I know you do...'

'I can't——' her hands hovered helplessly in mid-air, '—these gloves, I'll mark you——'

'You already have, indelibly. Touch me,' he commanded huskily, sealing her hesitation with his mouth and she gave in to the need, her gloves catching and pulling at his shirt as she slid her arms around him, up under the tailored jacket, digging her fingers into the rippling heat of his back. When next he raised his head she was trembling against him, her eyes wide and dark with unsated pleasure.

'Oh, yes, you missed me,' he growled with thick satisfaction, and Fran stirred, briefly unsettled by that possessive triumph. But when the warm hands supporting her shoulders slid down to press her shifting hips against the slow rotation of his her resentment died. He, too, was possessed by this blissful torment.

'I wasn't going to wait much longer, Frankie,' he told her, nipping the vulnerable curve of her throat. 'If you hadn't called me some time in the next couple of weeks, I would have come looking.'

'But, you said——'

'I know what I said.' He gave her a small shake. 'I was angry, the way you meant me to be, and my pride was suffering...but you were just being you, resisting the pitfalls of impulse, dealing with one problem at a time. I knew how critical it was to your self-respect that you make this business of yours a success. I estimated it would take you about four months to find your feet, to gain the confidence to look around and reassess your priorities. I made a pact with myself to let you have that time, without the added pressure of my presence. Of course, I didn't know you were going to let Beth in where you feared to let *me* tread...' He stroked his thumb across her lips in wry reproach.

'Beth is different——'

'I should hope so.'

She blushed. 'I mean, she really did need me.

His smile was sombre. 'So do I. Are you happy, Fran? Fulfilled? Or have you found out that success, alone, isn't enough to fill all the lonely crevices in your life?'

'I...I was going to ring you.' She owed him the confession. 'I was afraid you——' He laid a gentle finger across her lips, stopping her rush of words.

'It doesn't matter now. What matters is whether you're willing to make room for me in this brave new world of yours.'

'I think you already know the answer to that.' It was written in every line of the supple body shaped to his.

'I need to hear it, as much as you need to say it. What do you really want, Fran?'

'You.' There was exquisite relief in saying it at last, and a glorious sense of breaking free. 'I want a lover to share myself with...'

'Then you shall have him, Princess!' If he had been triumphant before, he was exultant now. 'And more...everything you ever wanted.' More? How could she want more than this heady feeling of freedom?

'You didn't sell the cabin, after all, did you?' he teased irrelevantly.

'I . . . no . . . I just mortgaged it and sold the rest. How did you know?'

'Because my intermediary made the outrageously generous offer that you refused for "sentimental reasons".' He laughed at her blush. 'It kept me going, through the lonely nights, knowing that you wanted to hold on to a piece of our memories. Now we can renew them. I can't think of a better place for a honeymoon, if we can keep my family at bay . . .'

'Honeymoon?' she echoed faintly and he grinned, misunderstanding her shock.

'Isn't marriage the guarantee that you wouldn't ask for, and I wouldn't give? I wasn't ready then . . . I was too hung up on saving face. But it's yours for the asking now . . .'

Marriage? To Ross? A lifetime of playing Russian roulette, wondering when her happiness was going to explode in her face? Fran went weak at the thought.

'Isn't it a bit too soon to be talking about marriage?' She strove for teasing lightness. 'Can't we just enjoy what we have for a while before we get serious?'

To her dismay he must have heard the buried note of panic. He drew back slightly, his eyes solidifying from melting warmth to blue ice at what he saw in her face. 'I thought we *were* serious. I thought that's what the fuss was about . . . you and I, having to readjust our lives to one another. Was I wrong? Exactly what *do* you think we have, Fran? What is it we should "just enjoy"?'

She stared, afraid to answer, feeling her brief moment of freedom slipping inexorably away. Oh, why were they always out of step? Why did he always insist on demanding more than she felt capable of giving?

'I see...you're dooming us before we even begin, aren't you, Fran?' he said bleakly. 'You'll trust me in your life, but only so far. You want a stud, not a lover. The hell of it is I'm almost tempted.'

'That's not fair, Ross!' Fran cried shakily, freeing herself from the fingers bruising her shoulders. 'Damn it, you spring this on me from nowhere...you said...we never even...marriage was never one of the options!'

'Nor is it now. It's the *only* one.'

Fran couldn't believe it. The conversation had the quality of a weird nightmare. 'But *why*? I thought you only wanted——'

'A slick exchange of sexual pleasures?' he cut in crudely. 'I could have got that from half a dozen women in the last few months.' He saw her wince and that seemed to enrage him even more. 'Do you think I'd have wasted all this time if all I wanted from you was *sex*! And you were willing to *settle* for that?' His incredulous disgust made her bewildered and angry. Just when she had reconciled herself to the rules of the game, he changed them. How did she know that he wouldn't change them again? 'My God, Fran, is that a measure of your own self-worth...or mine? It's an insult to both of us. What in the hell do you *want* from me? You obviously want something I'm not offering. Is it love? I wouldn't be here if I *wasn't* in love with you! You think I'd put myself through this kind of hell just for masochistic kicks? I love you, Francesca. Does that make a difference? Does that make me a better risk for your cautious soul?'

No! Fran's heart squeezed in anguish. Ross, in love with her? Dare she believe it? And if she did, what an awesome burden of responsibility it would be. His expectations of her were so impossibly high...he expected her to be herself, no barriers, no defences, *herself*, vulnerable to deepest joy and deepest hurt. Oh, God, she would disappoint him, she didn't think she could be that open. Her own suffering she had learned to cope with, but to know that *his* happiness rested with her...

Her hesitation was fatal. The blue flame that had burned so intensely in his eyes flickered and went out. Fran was stricken with the knowledge that already she had let him down. She put out a hand to touch him, wanting to explain, but he had already moved away, distancing himself with space as well as his heart-shattering words,

'No, I can see that it doesn't. I misjudged you, Francesca. It's not only giving love that you're afraid of, it's receiving it. And, coward that you are, I don't think it's a fear that you even *want* to conquer...'

CHAPTER TEN

WHAT am I *doing* here?

The roar inside Francesca's head was almost as loud as the booming rush of air past the open cabin door of the Cessna. Turning her head, weighted by her yellow helmet, she could see the young man sitting stiffly on the vibrating floor beside her. His eyes behind his goggles were tightly closed, his lips moving soundlessly. Fran wondered whether he was repeating the liturgy of the drill or a prayer. She had already said her prayers.

The other three first-time parachutists from her course were sitting in front of them, in the space left by the removal of the plane's passenger seats, facing the jump-master kneeling by the door. All too soon they would be over the drop zone and that sergeant-major bawl would be launching them into blue oblivion.

Why on earth am I here?

Because I'm crazy, the answer came. Crazy about a man who was crazy enough to do this for *fun*! Crazy enough to want to understand him, and, through him, herself. Crazy enough to do something drastic about it. This was a proving ground, a test and, if she could con-front and conquer this ultimate fear she knew that all others would dwindle in comparison. Heartbreak, rejec-tion, loss...after this she would know she could endure anything.

Poor Beth, she was justifiably bewildered by the events of the past couple of weeks. She had been flabbergasted to emerge from her bedroom that night to find her brother and her flatmate, not locked in impassioned embrace, but silently smouldering at each other from opposite sides of the room. Breakfast the next morning had been spent trying to ferret out the reason.

'Ross nearly bit my head off last night, when I asked him. He was in a foul mood all evening. I pity the poor woman whose baby he got dragged off to deliver half-way through the meal! What happened, I thought you two were nutty about each other?'

'Whatever gave you that idea?' said Fran automatically, staring into her coffee, alternately seething and despairing. How dared he give her something precious with one hand and snatch it away with the other! And because his ego was dented they were further apart now than they had ever been, even during the last few months of limbo that she had discovered last night *he* had decided she needed. And now he wanted to make another decision about *her* life!

'Come off it, Fran,' Beth scoffed. 'I've been in love hundreds of times, I recognise the signs, and I'm not so dumb that I don't know that my being Ross's sister had a lot to do with you letting me move in. Why do you think Mum was so keen? Ross told her he'd fallen for you, that's why. You just needed a little help in getting together——' She subsided, looking so guilty that Fran smiled wanly.

'It's all right. I did manage to figure out that last night wasn't just a startling coincidence.'

'Are you going to chuck me out?' Beth gnawed her lip.

'No, of course not, as long as you promise not to interfere again.'

'Cross my heart,' Beth vowed, but was unable to resist the desire to speculate, 'Did he try and talk you into an affair? Is that why you had a fight? Don't worry, Fran, he'll come round. You can't blame him for being twitchy, though, even if he is in love with you. Women have been trying to back him into corners for years, it's just a conditioned reflex to duck. Believe me, Mum wouldn't approve of Ross messing you around. She really likes you, she wouldn't want you to get hurt. She really thinks that Ross is serious about you——'

It was no use. Fran couldn't let Ross's family go on believing him the villain of the piece when he was being so disgustingly, implacably *honourable*...

'Well, you can set your mother's mind at rest...or I will when I write to her next. It's not Ross who's baulking at marriage. It's me.'

Beth was predictably scandalised. 'Fran!' she screamed, upsetting her coffee. 'He *proposed*? And you turned him *down*?' She hooted. 'Poor Ross, no wonder he looked as if he'd been run over by a concrete mixer!' Then outrage conquered sisterly malice. 'But *why*? Are you *crazy*? I thought you liked us, I thought you'd jump at the chance to be my sister-in-law,' she wailed.

'You marry a person, Beth, not a family,' Fran said drily, although she knew that wasn't quite the case with the Tarrants. They were all lovingly close.

'But what's the matter with Ross? Was it the way he asked or something?'

'Or something,' Fran sipped her coffee broodingly. 'And he didn't ask, he assumed.'

'You can't blame him for that,' said Beth uncertainly, 'I mean...he's got a lot to be confident about, don't you think? He loves you, he's disgustingly eligible, he's kind to children and animals, has a terrific respect for your career. What else could you *want*?' Put like that, it did sound incredible.

'He also likes dangerous sports,' Fran pointed out defensively. 'Specifically, jumping out of aeroplanes in mid-air.'

'Nobody's perfect,' Beth joked. Then, seeing Fran was deadly serious, she protested, 'But, Fran, that accident was a fluke. Statistically speaking, he's far more likely to be killed in a car accident. Or die of cancer, but I bet you wouldn't let *that* hold you back. If parachuting was really that dangerous, do you think Ross would encourage me to take it up? Yet when I was watching him jump last week he helped me sign up for——'

'He's jumping again?' Fran interrupted blindly, and Beth groaned.

'Oh, hell, me and my big mouth! Three times and text-book perfect every time. It's too late to worry now. What you don't know doesn't hurt you.'

She was wrong. Ignorance was the major cause of Fran's fear. By Ross's side or a thousand miles away, Fran was going to worry. Instead of letting her imagination run riot in the dark she should arm herself to the teeth with knowledge. Knowledge was power, knowledge was strength. Already she had let her insecurities dominate her to the point where they were ruling her life.

Beth was right about something else, though. It *was* more likely that Ross would be hurt in an accident on the road than anywhere else, but because Fran drove and accepted that risk herself her fears were proportionately less. An idea, wild and audacious, and worthy of Ross himself, took hold. Why should not the same perspective apply at a higher level of risk, too?

Ross loved her—enough to offer marriage, enough to offer secret assistance by trying to buy the cabin she had flung on to the market in a fit of defiance when the probate was finally settled. She couldn't even drum up any anger at the attempted manipulation, not when she knew it had been motivated by the sweetest of sentiments, the same ones that had led her to take the cabin off the market again barely two weeks later, admitting she would rather mortgage herself to the hilt than sever that precious link with love and Ross Tarrant. And if she loved him, didn't she owe him the best? A woman who was his equal, not one who let doubts and anxieties nibble away at the foundations of love until it crumbled into nothingness. Could she do it? Escape her own limitations, try her wings, literally, to see how high she could soar?

But when she blurted out her idea to Beth, instead of looking suitably impressed by her courage, the girl had been dubious. 'Do you think that's such a good idea? I mean...it's not really your kind of thing...'

'Is that a polite way of calling me a wimp?' Fran's jaw shot out even as Beth hurriedly denied the calumny. Ross had called her a coward too, once too often! She would do it, and to hell with what *they* thought!

'When's the next course?' she demanded, adding grimly when she saw Beth bite her lip, 'And don't you go running to Ross about this. I don't want him to know.'

'But then, I don't see the point——'

'No more meddling, Beth. You *promised*!'

'OK, but I tell you—I think you're crazy!'

That made the verdict unanimous. Christina, too, thought her friend insane.

'I get palpitations when the kids ride their bikes up to the shops, for goodness' sake,' she said, which only served to confirm Fran's theory about perspective. One loves, one fears...it was just necessary to get a proper handle on them, and not impose them constantly on others.

The hardest part, during the two weeks it took for Fran to rack up the required hours of ground-training at the parachute club was resisting the temptation, at Beth's urging, to ring Ross.

'At least give him some hope...tell him you're thinking about it. Please, Fran. He won't ring, you know. A man has his pride, after all, especially when he's just had his love and honour thrown back in his teeth as if they were insults!'

Fran had winced, but she hadn't given in to the emotional blackmail. Besides, Ross wasn't the kind of man to cave in at the first sign of resistance or adversity. If he loved her, he would be back...after his pride had given her the opportunity to stew for a while, by which time she would either have been tempered in her trial by fire or consumed by it. All or nothing, that was what he had demanded and that was what she was going to give him. If she wasn't strong enough to love him, she must be strong enough to reject him. Ironically, acceptance of her own weakness would require the greatest show of strength.

'OK?' The jumpmaster's voice was suddenly loud in her ear as he helped her into position sitting on the door sill, her legs dangling into a seventy-mile-per-hour slipstream. She had hardly been aware of the others jumping, but she could see them now, below her, five flowering canopies drifting on the light breeze.

'Go!'

Instantly obeying the command to go had been drilled into them so often that it was second nature. Fran went.

She pushed off firmly, collapsing into the solid pressure of the air two and a half thousand feet above mother earth. Without even thinking about it she went straight into the drill, forcing her body into the 'stable' position, stomach down arms and legs spreadeagled, head back against her pack as she shouted out the vital count, 'One thousand, two thousand, three thousand, four thousand. Check!'

Even before she had finished counting off the seconds she felt the disorientating jolt that pulled her into a vertical position, indicating that the static line attached to the plane had deployed her parachute. On the word 'check' she looked up to make sure and to her horror she saw that the canopy was billowing out into two asymmetrical lobes rather than a reassuring roundness. She recognised it instantly from their lectures as a 'Mae West'; one of the rigging lines must have caught over the top of the canopy. She looked down towards the other jumpers to judge her speed, and her stomach swooned as she realised that her descent was far more rapid than theirs. She was also starting to rotate in the rigging and knew that it would continue to increase at an alarming rate if she didn't act quickly. *Time*, it had been hammered into them, *is your biggest enemy*. Fran, with years of practice at reacting quickly to emergency situations, had performed the equipment and safety drills meticulously in class and now she automatically went into action, cold clarity of thought smothering her momentary sense of panic.

She reached for the handle on the top of the reserve parachute strapped to her stomach and pulled, holding the pack steady with her other hand and keeping her feet pressed tightly together. The handle came away and she let it go, grabbing the emerging reserve with both hands and throwing it violently down and away. It blossomed up past her, immediately slowing her rate of descent, and she rested her forearms on the reserve rigging lines to keep it clear of the main 'chute which was now beginning to collapse completely. A few seconds later she used the canopy releases to jettison the useless main, and watched it snake groundwards.

She had done it! She had only a brief moment of glorious relief to savour the drifting weightlessness, the beautiful sound of the canopy singing its rushing song of flight, before she was looking for the ground instructor, grasping the steering toggles to obey his hand signals to run and hold according to her position over the target area.

She didn't have time to be scared, even when the ground came streaking up at her—she was too busy. She tucked her arms up, bent her chin on to her chest and rounded her back, holding her knees and feet together to absorb the passive blow from the grassy field, and dissipating the shock of landing with a backward roll to the left.

She was scarcely aware of the congratulations of the instructor as she deflated her canopy and gathered it in, or of the excited chatter of her fellow students. Her hands shook as she removed her goggles. Dimly she heard someone say, 'You did everything right, Francesca, everything right. Here, let's get this off you and you can sit down.' Calm hands unbuckled her harness webbing and pulled off her helmet. 'Are you OK?'

And then there was another voice, abrupt, familiar, aggressively controlled. 'No, she's not OK, she's in shock. I'll look after her, I'm a doctor,' and she was being hustled across the uneven grass, half-dragged, half-carried, past the knot of interested friends and relations and Saturday-morning tourists, through the sagging farm gate to the road where a cluster of cars were parked. She was thrust on to the back seat of the nearest, a long, black limousine which even had a uniformed chauffeur sitting glassily in the front seat, her booted feet scuffing the roadside dust as her head was thrust unceremoniously between her knees. One of the jumpers must have some very rich and very vulgar friends, Fran thought with a semi-hysterical giggle. She stared at the Italian leather shoes, toe-to-toe in the dust with her borrowed boots.

Ross! Her shock began to dissipate as she realised that he must have witnessed her spectacular victory over self. Beth must have spilled the beans after all, but no matter, it saved Fran a trip. She felt drunk with relief. She wanted to share the bubbling exhilaration with Ross. For a few minutes up there she had walked the knife-edge, thrilled to the sharp taste of fear. But this time, unlike that terrifying flight in the Tiger Moth, she had been prepared for it . . . had conquered the fear with her own force of will. It was like a revelation, illuminating all the shadowy corners of her psyche. Fran knew now that she could conquer the world if she wanted to . . . !

'Ross——'

'Shut up and breathe!' The hand tightened murderously on her neck and Fran squeaked. His tone of voice was hardly calculated to soothe her shock. Wasn't he going to congratulate her? He had toasted Beth with champagne! Fran hadn't gone to watch her friend's inaugural jump, not only because she wasn't ready to face Ross, whom she knew would be there, but because she thought that it would be a psychologically disastrous move to confront the reality of what all those ground drills meant until the last possible moment. Coward to the last . . . but a brave one!

'Ross——'

Suddenly the weight lifted from her neck and she was hauled upright, dangling on tiptoe from the jumpsuit fabric balled in his fists. She gulped as she got her first look at his expression. Congratulations were definitely not on his agenda! He looked grey under his tan, the sexy mouth clamped into a thin line, his eyes two chips of blue steel.

'What in the bloody *hell* were you doing up there?' His snarl took the skin off the top of her ears and she stared at him open-mouthed. The instructor had been pleased. Had Ross's expert eye seen something that he had missed?

'It all happened so fast,' she gasped apologetically, trying to loosen his grip with unsteady hands. 'Should I have tried to clear the canopy? I didn't think there was time to have a go and we were told that if there's any doubt——'

'Not *that*!' he roared, shaking her furiously. 'You know damned well what I mean. I mean, what were you doing up there *at all*? And don't try and feed me that lie you fed Beth about it having nothing to do with me. It has *everything* to do with me. You never showed any sign of being interested in adventure sports before. Why now? What incredibly cretinous theory about us have you cooked up in that tiny little brain that makes you think you have to *prove* anything to me? Goddammit, Frankie, have you any idea what I went through when I saw that malfunction? Well?' he rattled her again. 'Have you?'

The adrenalin still rushing frantically around her body was well shaken up by this time. 'No, but I can make a good guess,' she threw at him. 'At least I didn't land in a tree and break every bone in my body.'

'*What* did you say?' he asked, in a thick and dangerous voice and Fran, still feeling cocky, started to repeat herself with pointed sweetness. She didn't get past the first word. He kissed her with the full force of his anger and, after a moment of recoil from his savagery, Fran kissed him back, with equal force. She was his equal, in every way, and she was through running away from the prospect of loving him.

He broke the kiss as violently as he had begun it, one hand lifting from her shoulder to wipe his mouth. They both stared at the blood which streaked the hard knuckles.

'Is that yours, or mine?' Fran asked shakily and Ross closed his eyes, and shuddered. 'You're not going to faint at the sight of a little blood are you, Doctor?' she murmured as he actually swayed on his feet. He made a raw sound and put his arms around her, not gently, holding her hard against the erratic beat of his heart.

'Don't you ever, *ever*, do that to me again,' he said with quiet violence.

'Parachute?' Fran asked, her voice muffled in his chest. Now that her initial shock and euphoria had died she was realising that she didn't particularly want to make a habit of this kind of thing.

'Shut me out of a decision like this. I need to know, I need to be part of it. Oh, Frankie, I accused you of being a coward, but I'm the coward here, not you. I dismissed your fears as of no account because I was afraid that I would lose you if I admitted that they had any validity. But they do. God, how could I have been such a hypocrite as to say that I love you and yet be willing to put you through the kind of agony I just went through? I never fully realised before how utterly terrifying it can be to watch someone you love hover literally between life and death and be powerless to help them. I had an inkling of it when you swam out to the boat that day, but I didn't know I was in love with you then. I didn't realise it until you walked out on me, and I faced the fact that it wasn't a matter of choice any more. I couldn't just shrug and let you go, I *had* to make you love me, even if it took the rest of my life. But you do, don't you, Fran?' His arms tightened briefly. 'That's *why* you were so afraid and now I understand... But you don't have to be any more. If you want me to give up this sort of thing, I will, with no regrets. I'd far rather have you, just the way you are. You don't have to make any grand gestures to show me how brave you are, I don't care. Just show me your love, that's bravery enough...if you can...'

'I didn't do this for you, Ross,' Fran said, with tender amusement at his anguished humility. 'I did it for me. I wasn't trying to be someone I'm not—just to be a strong *me*. And I am. I'm...free. I needed to know that I could trust myself before I could trust anyone else. And I do trust you, Ross. I know that you would never deliberately hurt me. So don't *you* make any grand gestures, either. Even if you never regretted giving up your racketing around the skies, *I* would.'

He caught his breath and cupped her face, lifting it from the cradle of his chest. The clear, grey serenity of her eyes smote him to the bone. Her love was there, open and unafraid, for him to see.

'Yes, I love you,' she said huskily and watched his skin flush with warmth.' All of you, not just the pieces that I feel comfortable with. And I couldn't bear it if you thought that you had to be less than you are for my sake.' She smiled at his expression. 'I want you to be more, not less. I love you, Ross.'

The long fingers tightened possessively on her jaw, his eyes alight with joy, relief. 'I thought you did, oh, God, I hoped you did, but how good it is to hear you say it. Do you know how wild it drove me trying to work out why the idea of marriage to me was so horrifying? Even if you didn't love me, I thought you'd at least be *flattered*...' His soft laugh held the memory of his frustrated anger. 'When I went to bed that night I was cursing Beth for jumping the gun and myself for greedily trying to take advantage of it. I had been so proud of my damned patience so far, and it all went out the window in a moment when you suddenly looked at me as if I'd sprouted horns, rather than the halo I thought I deserved. Such arrogance...'

'Magnificent arrogance,' she agreed mischievously and he laughed, this time with some of that same, beloved arrogance.

'Like a callow boy I was outraged that you didn't treat my love like the priceless gift it was, and spitefully I tried to make you feel guilty about it.'

'You succeeded.'

'You got your revenge. When I saw that 'Mae West' I thought it would be my fault if you died. That I'd driven you into believing you had to be some kind of Amazon to earn my respect. But that you always had, and always will...' He tilted his head to the sky and blurted out, 'I still can't believe you did that!'

'I wanted to see what it was like,' she said meekly.

His lips moved silently, very like those of her fellow parachutist before he went out the door. 'And what was it like?' he finally asked, in strangled tones.

'I don't really know, it all happened so fast,' she admitted sheepishly. 'Not as scary as I'd expected while everything was going on and then...sort of quiet but not quiet...rather awesome and fantastic...' Her enthusiasm died a little as she remembered what could have happened. '...I think...'

Ross felt the last of his tension drain away to be replaced by a heavy, sultry sensation of anticipation, spiked with delicious slivers of amusement.

'It gets better,' he said, but didn't make the mistake of grinning at the expression of horror that flitted across her face. No, he didn't have to worry about Fran acquiring an insatiable thirst for adventure, she would continue to express her own quiet courage in other ways. But he would make damned sure that it wasn't over-stretched. She had taught him a lesson that he couldn't unlearn and didn't want to. He frowned, realising that they still hadn't settled the question of marriage. After last time it wouldn't do to take too much for granted. That was another lesson he had learned well.

'Can I give you a lift back to town?'

'I think we're supposed to have a debriefing,' Fran said vaguely, looking around and realising that they were standing in the middle of a public road and that they were getting a few funny looks from the spectators now trailing back to their cars. She shrugged hurriedly out of the loose encirclement of his arms.

'I think I can take care of your debriefing,' Ross murmured with a wicked look downwards that made her tingle. 'Did you come in the club van with the others?' She nodded. 'Good, then there's no car to worry about.'

He put his hands flat against her shoulders and pushed. Startled, she fell backwards, on to the seat of the limousine she had sheltered in earlier.

'Ross, what do you think you're doing?' she hissed at him as he bent and scooped her legs into the car, thrusting her along the deep leather seat with a sinuous nudge of his hips as he joined her. 'You can't just commandeer——'

'Home, James,' Ross flicked the switch on the small intercom on the padded panel in front of them and the chauffeur, without looking back through the tinted panel of glass, made an acknowledging gesture with his hand as he leaned forward to start the car.

'Ross? Ross, this isn't *yours*, is it?' He was wearing a suit again she realised, on a *Saturday*—looking smooth and suave and stinking rich. She longed to see him in scruffy denims again . . . or in nothing at all.

He ignored her disbelieving squawk, punching up some numbers on a sleek, cordless phone. 'Nessa? I'm on my way home. Only urgent calls, please . . . Dr Nugent can take the rest.' He hung up. 'Nessa is my housekeeper. She picks up after me and generally nags me about life in general. Rather like you, in fact,' he added slyly, 'except she's thirty years older and doesn't drive me out of my skull with lust and desire and terrifying elusiveness.'

'I can't believe that you could be crass enough to drive around town in something like this,' Fran said severely, conscious of the man in the front seat, trying to hide the lurch of excitement she felt at seeing Ross leaning back against the cream upholstery, regarding her with that heavy-lidded sensual amusement. 'After all your sneers about the material trappings of success.'

'He can't hear you, Fran, or see you. All the glass is mirrored.' Ross judged her nervous glance accurately. He grinned lazily at her flush. 'And you're right, I'm not that crass. I rented this to take a very important, wealthy Middle-Eastern patient out to the airport this morning. Just one of the small touches of courtesy and luxury that she takes for granted. I was on my way back home when Beth called, in a panic because she hadn't been able to get hold of me and thought she was cutting it too fine——'

'She wasn't suppose to tell you at all.'

'Wasn't she?' he asked drily, and smiled as Fran's eyes flickered. Had she been setting some kind of test for him as well, without realising it? If so, he had passed with flying colours. 'Anyway, that's why I over-reacted so violently back there. I was shattered by nerves before we even got in sight of the drop zone. Beth said she'd told you about my jumps and you'd closed up and gone "all quiet and fanatical" about doing it yourself. I didn't know what to think. Add to that two speeding tickets and a near-miss with a roadside goat, and that "Mae West" was just a match to the powder keg. It was either beat you or kiss you senseless, and I couldn't do either I was shaking so much.'

Fran cleared her throat. 'The jumpmaster told us that lots of wives and girlfriends of the male jumpers often help as judges in sky-diving competitions. Perhaps I could do that... if I'm not up there myself, of course,' she added bravely to herself, making his mouth twitch.

'Of course,' he murmured. 'We'll wait and see, shall we?' He paused. 'As wife or girlfriend?'

She looked at him and he smiled reassuringly, but he forgot to guard his eyes, which had taken on that steely look again. 'Is that a choice?' asked Fran innocently.

'Yes.' And just as quickly, 'No.' He frowned, and looked unseeingly out at the passing fields. 'Yes. I don't know.' He shrugged impatiently and looked at her with brooding resentment. 'What do you want it to be?'

'What happened to the strong, decisive man I fell in love with?' she mourned gleefully. 'Who is this wishy-washy substitute?'

'*Wishy-washy?*' Suddenly she was flat on her back against the cool leather seat, laughingly pushing at his wide shoulders. 'You want decisive, Princess? I'll give you decisive——'

And he was kissing her, devouring her with lips and teeth and tongue, and while she was dealing with the erotic shock of his mouth on hers his hands were busily unzipping her flight suit and burrowing eagerly under the tracksuit she wore underneath. The purring hum of the powerful car beneath her, and the tigerish growl of the big man on top of her combined in an exquisite inner vibration that burned from her belly to her brain. He swore roughly at the tangle her clothing created and rolled sideways the better to deal with it, so that they both lay slanted on the seat, their legs entwining, feet jammed against the panelled wood of the door.

'Ross, wait——' Fran shuddered as he found the hard peak of her breast and stroked it lovingly through her silky, seamless bra, making it swell and harden even further.

'I've done nothing else but, since I met you, and if you get pregnant you'll *have* to damned well marry me——'

'I only wanted to say yes.'

'Yes what?' he muttered vaguely, tasting her skin with a connoisseur's appreciation and a starving man's fervour.

'Yes, I'll marry you, even if I *don't* get pregnant.'

'Of course you will,' he purred, moving his hand down her body, pushing under the soft waistband of her tracksuit pants and touching her with mind-bending gentleness and intimacy. 'Your compassionate heart couldn't bear to condemn me to a lifetime of painful frustration. God——' his hips flexed involuntarily as her thigh dragged against his swollen hardness with a convulsive jerk of pleasure, '—you're so hot and sweet and ready for me...how in the hell are we going to work this?' He groaned as he rubbed himself against her, building the pressure for release as he tried to wrestle her out of the restricting jumpsuit.

'Ross, you do remember where we are, don't you?'

'How could I forget?' He cursed as he realised he had no chance of getting the suit off while she still had her boots on.

'Don't you think we should wait for a more appropriate time and place?' Fran asked, quivering with love and laughter at his passionate antics.

'What could be more appropriate, Princess?' he growled. 'We've come full circle. Here we are again, trying to make love in the back seat of a car...except this time we know precisely what we're doing, and why, and nothing and no one is going to separate us again...'

Full circle. A circle of love without beginning or end, and large enough to encompass every dream that Francesca could ever wish for. She began to help him, eagerly...

The Perfect Gift.

Four new exciting novels from Mills and Boon:

SOME SORT OF SPELL – by Frances Roding
– An enchantment that couldn't last or could it?

MISTRESS OF PILLATORO – by Emma Darcy
– The spectacular setting for an unexpected romance.

STRICTLY BUSINESS – by Leigh Michaels
– highlights the shifting relationship between friends.

A GENTLE AWAKENING – by Betty Neels
– demonstrates the truth of the old adage 'the way to a man's heart…'

Make Mother's Day special with this perfect gift.
Available February 1988. Price: £4.80

From: Boots, Martins, John Menzies, W H Smith,
Woolworths and other paperback stockists.

Mills & Boon

YOU'RE INVITED TO ACCEPT **FOUR ROMANCES** AND A TOTE BAG **FREE!**

Acceptance card

| NO STAMP NEEDED | Post to: Reader Service, FREEPOST, P.O. Box 236, Croydon, Surrey. CR9 9EL |

Please note readers in Southern Africa write to:
Independant Book Services P.T.Y., Postbag X3010, Randburg 2125, S. Africa

YES! Please send me 4 free Mills & Boon Romances and my free tote bag – and reserve a Reader Service Subscription for me. If I decide to subscribe I shall receive 6 new Romances every month as soon as they come off the presses for £7.20 together with a FREE monthly newsletter including information on top authors and special offers, exclusively for Reader Service subscribers. There are no postage and packing charges, and I understand I may cancel or suspend my subscription at any time. If I decide not to subscribe I shall write to you within 10 days. Even if I decide not to subscribe the 4 free novels and the tote bag are mine to keep forever. I am over 18 years of age   EP20R

NAME _____

(CAPITALS PLEASE)

ADDRESS _____

_____

POSTCODE _____